"You still in your father's will?" Kevin asked.

Penny laughed. "Don't worry about my dad."

"Thanks for not introducing me as one of his cabana boys," Kevin said. "He'd have freaked. I probably would have gotten fired."

Penny's eyes blazed with anger. "It's so unfair. But you've got nothing to worry about. He has no idea who you are."

Kevin nodded. "So, um, maybe I should keep a low profile. Make sure I don't call attention to myself if he happens to be walking around and shaking hands. Which means maybe we shouldn't be seen together out here."

Penny sighed. "I'm not letting him control me that way. My dad has his own ideas about which guys I should see. Ken dolls with sculpted hair showing Ivy League roots. Anyone else need not apply. But I have my own ideas too. He and I spar. It's no big deal."

"Maybe not to you," Kevin said. "But I have to be careful. Or I could lose my job."

"You know," she said. "We sort of got interrupted last night during a key moment."

Kevin grinned. "I think I know what key moment you're referring to."

Penny turned to the left, then to the right. No one could see them. She stepped close to him. He stepped even closer. And this time *he* kissed *her*.

Brothers Trilogy

Kevin

ZOE ZIMMERMAN

BANTAM BOOKS
NEW YORK · TORONTO · LONDON · SYDNEY · AUCKLAND

RL: 6, AGES 012 AND UP

KEVIN

A Bantam Book / June 2000

Cover photography by Michael Segal.

Produced by 17th Street Productions,
an Alloy Online, Inc. company.
33 West 17th Street
New York, NY 10011.

ISBN: 0-553-49323-X

Visit us on the Web! www.randomhouse.com/teens

Published simultaneously in the United States and Canada

Bantam Books is an imprint of Random House Children's Books, a
division of Random House, Inc. BANTAM BOOKS and the rooster
colophon are registered trademarks of Random House, Inc. Bantam Books,
1540 Broadway, New York, New York 10036.

PRINTED IN THE UNITED STATES OF AMERICA

OPM   0 9 8 7 6 5 4 3 2 1

One

FIFTEEN-YEAR-OLD KEVIN FORD was dreaming of girls in bikinis. Tall girls. Short girls. Blondes. Brunettes. Redheads. Girls frolicking on the beach, their tanned bods glistening in the sun and smelling irresistibly of cocoa butter—

"Yo."

Kevin ignored the familiar voice and smiled as he drifted back into the dream. A redhead in cutoffs and a flowered bikini top was asking him to rub suntan lotion on her attractively freckled back. . . .

"Yo," came the voice again, this time accompanied by a toe jabbing Kevin's ribs.

"What?" Kevin growled at his eldest brother, Johnny, not daring to open his eyes and face the morning. But he knew what. Time to get up. Time to go to work for the rich people. Time to stop dreaming—which was exactly what hanging out on the beach with hot girls *was* for a working stiff like Kevin.

"We're gonna be late," Johnny warned as he headed toward the kitchen in his Calvin Klein briefs. "You shower first."

"Uh-huh," Kevin mumbled, rising to a sitting position on the uncomfortable brown couch. The apartment the three Ford brothers had rented in Surf City, California for the summer had only two bedrooms. Which meant that for one month out of the three, one Ford brother had to sleep on the couch while the other two enjoyed the comfort of a real bed. Kevin's other brother, Danny, had taken the couch for the month of June. Once July 1 hit, it was Kevin's turn.

It wasn't so bad, Kevin figured. At least he could fall asleep to the TV.

He stretched and watched Johnny shove a pair of Pop-Tarts into the toaster. Johnny had been waking up Kevin the same way every morning since the summer began and they both started working at the Surf City Resort Hotel (Johnny as a lifeguard, Kevin as a cabana boy). Yep, that was older bro Johnny: seventeen years old, preparing for college, responsible, practical, with a mind for money and how to make it. Johnny was always the one waking everyone else up.

"Time to earn your rent, kid," Johnny announced, yanking the cap on a jug of milk.

Money, money, money, Kevin mused. *Always money.* "Yeah," he replied. "If I get any more one-dollar tips, I just might have to retire."

"Hey, it's a job, Kevin," Johnny reminded him. "It lets us live in this wonderful little kingdom for the summer. And if you bust your butt, you might have some cash left over for the school year."

"Are you kidding?" Kevin shot back as he stood up and folded his blanket. "We're gonna have ten grand burning a hole in our well-lined pockets by the end of the summer."

Kevin was referring to their entire reason for existence: the Surf City 3-on-3 Beach Volleyball Tournament, sponsored by Fizz Cola. It was held every August at the Surf City Resort Hotel. The grand prize: ten thousand dollars and a lifetime supply of Fizz Cola.

That money was a huge carrot hanging in front of the Ford brothers' noses as they trudged to work every morning. Especially Johnny's. He was planning on using his share for college, which was right around the corner for him. In fact, Kevin figured that Johnny wasn't just *hoping* to win the cash, but *planning* on it. He was driven to go to college and land a good job so he could make some good green. The American dream and all that.

It wasn't that Johnny was all about the money, Kevin knew. It was a simple fact of economics. The Fords didn't come from much. Their dad was a plumber, with a collar as blue as the Pacific sky outside their window, and their mom was a housewife. Mr. Ford did what he could for his three boys. But unlike many of their friends' situations, college wasn't a sure thing for the Ford brothers. Johnny knew what it meant to be the first person in the family to go. He also knew what it meant to get a good job. But Kevin wished Johnny could let go of his obsession once in a while and just have a good time.

"Toss me that volleyball." Johnny gestured at the ball resting in an open, empty pizza box a few feet from Kevin.

Kevin spun it back with his toe, rolled it up his shin, caught it, and tossed it to his brother. "What gives?"

An evil smile broke across Johnny's face. "Time to wake up the slacker." He marched down the hall toward the bedrooms.

Kevin went into the kitchen and found a crumpled box of Pop-Tarts with one pack left. As he tore into it, he heard a loud *whop!* as the volleyball smacked into Danny's closed bedroom door.

"Hey!" came Danny's tired voice.

"Wake up, slacker!" Johnny called. "Today's a beautiful day for job hunting."

Kevin chuckled, silently approving of Johnny's methods. Hey, he was all for a guy meeting a great gal and hanging out on the beach with her all summer. But since Danny had lost his job, it fell to Johnny and Kevin to pick up the financial slack. Which meant a lot of ramen noodles, Pop-Tarts, and minibar snacks stolen from the hotel.

"That's real mature, John," came Danny's irritated voice.

"You'd better get up and start looking for a job," Johnny said. "The two of us can't support you all summer."

Kevin munched his Pop-Tarts and smiled. If you asked sixteen-year-old Danny about money, he'd

4

say, *"Whatever."* Danny had gotten fired from his job as a waiter at Jabba's Palace—a greasy burger joint on the boardwalk—because he'd told off Jabba for discriminating against weirdos like his girl-friend, Raven. Okay, she wasn't a weirdo. But she did have a lot of pink strands in her hair, more ear-rings than Kevin could count, and somewhere on her black-clothed body, a tattoo.

So Kevin couldn't really criticize Danny. He might not have a job, but he was the only Ford brother to find a girlfriend this summer. And an in-teresting one at that.

"Dan, I don't hear you getting up," Johnny called out. He bounced the volleyball against the door again, then came back into the kitchen.

"Shut up, Johnny," came Danny's gruff voice. "Sleeping until noon does *not* cause cancer!"

"He's got you there," Kevin said as Johnny re-filled his glass of milk.

Johnny threw the empty box of Pop-Tarts at Kevin, then grinned. "Shut up and get ready."

The phone rang, and Johnny snatched the re-ceiver.

"Hello? Oh, hey, Raven. Yeah, he's up, but barely. Hang on." Johnny pressed the receiver against his chest and turned to Kevin. "Go tell the slacker his girlfriend's on the phone."

Kevin headed off to Danny's bedroom. The middle Ford brother sure had it lucky. No job *and a* girlfriend. Kevin figured if he had to have a job, he deserved a grade-A girlfriend to hang out with too.

5

Yeah. A girlfriend. Now, that would make this summer a lot more fun. And checking out the babes lining the pool at the Surf City Resort Hotel would make his pathetic *job* a lot more fun too.

Johnny and Kevin rode their bikes down the boardwalk in silence. There wasn't much to talk about. They did this ride every morning, same time, same channel. The same stands and shops flitted by. Morning joggers and power walkers passed, arms pumping. Kevin figured it must be nice for the renters who came in for only a week. For them Surf City really was a change of scenery and pace. But for him the only thing that changed was the movie-theater marquee. He'd drawn it all a thousand times over.

Man, what it would be like to not have to work, he thought, his feet mindlessly pedaling. *Just to be able to chill. Just to draw.*

That's all he wanted to do. Just draw. He did it all the time in his mind, on napkins, in his sketch-book. His brothers and teachers thought he was pretty good (at least they said so). But the problem with wanting to devote your life to creating art was finding time to create said art. It was so unfair that Kevin's one true passion had to take a backseat to living, eating, sleeping, and, worst of all, working.

Working is the destroyer of all things artistic, Kevin thought bitterly. *People have no appreciation of beauty and what it takes to create it.*

How could he create anything great when he spent all his time delivering towels at a hotel? *Grrr.*

6

In a cool world the artist would be king.

That was the dream of every artist, Kevin figured. If he could get some real time, maybe then he could find something truly interesting as a subject. Take his time. Do it up right.

As it was now, Kevin's drawing was limited to lunch breaks and the occasional hour or two on the weekend. And that bonus time was generally spent lounging on the beach, so what he ended up drawing was waves or boats or babes.

Not that each subject didn't present its own challenge (especially the girls, for which Kevin thought he had a real affinity). But how many surf scenes could one man draw?

Trying to work on lunch hour was a nightmare as well. He no longer drew in public, so finding an isolated spot to scarf some food and scribble some lines was the real challenge. That and trying not to get any food on the sketch pad.

Once, while on break, he sat near the pool to draw. A rich, middle-aged woman wearing full-blown makeup and jewelry while in her bathing suit (her feet never touched the water of the pool or the sand of the beach) gazed over his shoulder to see what he was doing. When he paused for her reaction, she literally looked down her nose at his work—so much so that her eyes crossed slightly—and sniffed. "A young man shouldn't waste his time doodling," she'd said.

"Some people get paid a lot of money to doodle," Kevin replied cheerfully.

The muscles in the woman's jaw flexed angrily. "The art world is full of phonies and swindlers. I'm from New York, young man. Trust me. I *know*. You shouldn't waste your time on it. You'll never make a living selling drawings. Stick with the basics, young man. Accounting and marketing. If you can do either, you can go a long way in this world."

Ugh, he thought. *She has to be kidding. Yeah, that's just what the world needs: another soulless robot hanging from a rung on the corporate ladder.*

Kevin didn't bother arguing that there were so many other possibilities in the art world: design, computer graphics; the list was endless. Drawing was just the beginning. And he had just turned fifteen. He had some time before the college alarm bells sounded.

But he did hear the clock ticking. . . .

How could he miss it? Johnny constantly talked about college and constantly rode Danny about his apathy toward it. Johnny just couldn't understand how Danny didn't know what he wanted to do with his life. Johnny knew from the beginning. He was lucky.

Kevin figured he was lucky too. He'd drawn since he was a kid. He never really doubted that it would somehow figure into whatever he did for a career.

Ha! Career.

Who was Kevin kidding? All he wanted to do was chill out and draw.

Just then he and Johnny passed a gorgeous female in spandex running tights and wraparound shades, with a bouncing ponytail. Both Ford brothers turned to watch her go down the boardwalk.

"Yow," Johnny said.

"Yeah," Kevin replied.

Then they returned their attention to the ride.

Beautiful women were everywhere in Surf City. And the one who just ran by them only served to remind Kevin how lonely he really had become that summer. It was July, for crying out loud. He hadn't met *anyone*. Johnny had Jane, his steady girl from home. Danny had Raven. But what about the Kevster?

Who wants to date a cabana boy? he wondered. None of the rich daddy's girls who populated the poolside at the hotel, that was for sure. They were too busy chatting on their cell phones about shopping or modeling or their boyfriends' trust funds. As stunningly gorgeous as they were—and they were ten-Porsche-pileup gorgeous—Kevin couldn't stand them.

Well, maybe he could stand them for one date. At least they were very nice to look at.

Other than those 150-dollar-jean queens, Kevin's exposure to the fairer sex was limited. If they didn't work or stay at the hotel, Kevin didn't have time to meet them. And even if they did, he still didn't have time (more towels, kid!).

Gradually the Surf City Resort Hotel came into view up ahead, rising from the boardwalk like some faux Greek ruin recently restored by Donald Trump. Two massive wings—twenty floors of guest rooms—fanned out from a grand central atrium rising to a glass ceiling inside the lobby of the hotel. The obnoxious fountain in front spewed endlessly into the air. Three restaurants served continental, Mexican, and seafood cuisine. The gift shop sold everything from Mentos to Armani suits. In the back of the hotel a huge patio gave way to an even more huge two-tiered pool with a swim-up bar. Beyond that was the hotel's private beach and the ocean. Beyond that was a long swim to Hawaii.

This is my life, he thought glumly. *This is how I'm spending all my time. It just doesn't seem fair. Other kids come to the beach and have fun and find people to date. Me? I get to give them their towels.*

He and Johnny pulled up and locked their bikes on a rack at the rear of the hotel where another dozen employees' bikes were stashed. Johnny said, "Later," and headed toward the beach and his lifeguard stand.

Oh, well. No use complaining anymore.

Time to go to work. Where he could forget about finding his grade-A girlfriend.

TWO

B Y NOON KEVIN had delivered several dozen
towels and chaise cushions to the poolside,
schlepped five brunch orders for room service, and
swept up a broken lemonade pitcher. By lunchtime
the pool and private beach always filled to capacity,
so much of Kevin's time was spent running back
and forth and trying not to get his white Surf City
Resort polo shirt and shorts splashed by the little
brats in their two-hundred-dollar swim trunks.

"Yes, sir, right away. I'll have your towel in two
shakes."

"No, ma'am, they don't allow the chaise cushions in
the pool. I can get your son an inflatable raft if you want."

"More soda for you . . . water for you . . . margaritas
for you?"

All the same. Mindless.

Kevin took a fifteen-minute break around one.
He gulped a bottle of spring water at the bar near

the pool, eyeing a particularly attractive girl in a red bikini rubbing suntan oil on her arms. Her long, blond hair was done up in a ponytail, her toes were painted red to match her swimsuit, and her shades probably cost five hundred dollars.

"Can't you read the sign, kid?" a big man warned, clapping him on the back. "No drooling."

Kevin recognized the voice immediately and smirked. "I'm on break. The rules don't apply when you're on break."

Jake Hackman slid in next to him at the bar, signaling for a water bottle of his own. Jake was Kevin's boss. His title was assistant executive manager or some such, but Kevin couldn't keep track. He just knew Jake as "the boss," the thirty-something guy who was in charge of the cabana boys, the waiters and waitresses, and the maid service. Like every employee of the hotel, Jake was clean-cut and bright eyed. His dark hair and mirror shades gave him a sort of small-town–sheriff quality, but Jake was always cool to Kevin. And he was an expert at taking abuse from guests and transforming it into pleasantries and humble service. Sometimes Kevin didn't know how Jake did it.

"How's it going?" Jake asked.

"No problems," Kevin replied, smiling. "Just churning and burning those towels. We go through so many, you'd think the people were eating them."

"Fresh towels are like fresh flowers or fresh fruit," Jake commented. "They make people feel better. And they also give the impression of luxury and excess, which is what these people are paying for. Think about it. Say you go swimming, and when you get out of the pool, there's a nice, big, clean, fluffy towel waiting for you."

"Can't say that's ever happened to me," Kevin replied, snickering.

"You're hanging around the wrong people," Jake shot back, nudging him. "Maybe you should go ask out little Miss Whitcomb after all."

Kevin blinked. "Who?"

Jake nodded at the girl in the red bikini. "Emily Whitcomb, daughter of Frank and Doris Whitcomb and heir to a paper-towel fortune. She's here with Mommy and is *very* bored. Daddy's away on business, and most of Em's friends went on a summerlong backpacking trip across Southeast Asia."

Kevin laughed. "How do you know all that?"

"Come on, Kevster," Jake replied, scowling good-naturedly. "You have to open your ears. All that information is yours for the taking if you just listen. Little Emily spends most of her afternoons on a cell phone."

"That's eavesdropping," Kevin scolded, wagging a finger at Jake.

"That's classified," Jake said with a wink.

"She's out of my league anyway," Kevin added. "I'm holding out for a toilet-paper heiress."

Jake chuckled. "Well, forget about her anyway. You know the rules. No fraternizing with the guests. And that's right from the Man himself."

"Yeah, yeah, yeah," Kevin said, sipping his water.

"No self-respecting billionairess-in-waiting would be caught dead talking to a guy like me anyway."

"Unless she's ordering a diet soda and some towels," Jake replied. "In which case you jump like you have an electric eel in your shorts." He chugged some of his water and changed the subject. "How many hours you have in this week so far?"

"I'm averaging ten a day. Why?"

Jake shrugged. "Just making sure everyone's getting their fair share of abuse. By the way, you're lazy, disrespectful, and not worth the paper your paycheck is printed on. There. You have now had your fair share of abuse. Get back to work."

"Thanks, Jake," Kevin replied cheerfully. "Are you just doing that to impress Mr. Booth?"

"Say what?" Jake asked, puzzled.

"He's right over there," Kevin said, pointing at the intimidating-looking man who was shaking hands with guests by the bar.

Jake spied Mr. Booth and cocked an eyebrow at Kevin. "Of course, cabana maggot. Now, vamoose before I fire you so hard, the unemployment rate goes up in Japan."

"That's a good one, boss," Kevin replied, finishing his water. But his gaze was on Mr. Austin Booth: owner and operator of the Surf City Resort Hotel; a man who wore dark suits in ninety-degree sunshine even when he was visiting the pool area; a man known for his dour and curt dealings with his staff; a man who wasted no time in things that did not concern him (to the point of being aloof); a

14

man who ran several luxury hotels up and down the southern California coast, two more in Aspen, Colorado, and a five-star restaurant in Beverly Hills. Rumor had it that he played poker with Aaron Spelling, Jay Leno, and Tommy Lasorda once a week. Golf with Michael Douglas on weekends. A real LA heavyweight.

Mr. Booth wandered from guest to guest, greeting them, exchanging pleasantries. His suit was flawless. His tall, slim frame moved effortlessly as he shook and kissed hands like a dignitary. His smile was bright and sincere. Not one of his silver hairs was out of place.

"There's your first lesson on how to be a millionaire, Kevin," Jake pointed out.

"What's that?"

Jake smiled at him. "Schmoozing. Know how to talk to people. And more important, know who to talk to. Notice that Mr. Booth doesn't spend one second looking at or talking to the staff. It's as though the worker bees don't even exist." Jake finished his own water and set the bottle on the bar. "Did you know that the average millionaire doesn't take extravagant vacations, build extensive wine cellars, and buy yachts?"

"They don't?" Kevin asked.

Jake shook his head. "Their primary leisure-time activity is raising funds for charity, meeting with financial advisers, and consulting tax experts. That's a fact, Kev. Tuck it away and remember it."

Kevin smirked. "Why's that?"

"Because if you want to be wealthy," Jake replied, smoothly slipping away from the bar, "you have to know how to stay wealthy. Get back to work, young man."

Kevin grinned at his boss and nodded. *Whatever, Jake. Being wealthy isn't everything.*

Then Kevin watched as Austin Booth kissed the hand of the beautiful and bored Miss Emily Whitcomb. They chatted like old friends. And the only reason Austin Booth was doing that was because he owned a hotel that was luxurious enough to attract a rich young woman like Emily.

Hmmm, Kevin thought. *Maybe Jake is on to something after all.*

By three, Kevin was starting to poop out. He'd run hard all day as usual and was now operating on autopilot. The "yes, ma'ams" and "right aways" were robotic. On the bright side, his right-front pocket was stuffed with roughly twenty-five one-dollar bills, as well as a magical fiver from a rich old woman who wanted a pack of unfiltered Red Apples, a cigarette brand that the hotel didn't carry (not exactly what Kevin would've expected coming from this woman, who exuded the smell of money like perfume). He had to hump it down the boardwalk to a newsstand to find the brand. He was back in less than five minutes. The grateful woman passed him a crisp Abe Lincoln while she lit up.

That's about a max out on tips, he thought. He knew he wouldn't do much better on any given day. And it was now getting too late to think he'd net any more. The poolside was slowly growing deserted as the guests took refuge in their rooms to prepare for the evening meal.

Still, some guests remained. And they needed to be taken care of.

"Boy!" came an irritated female voice.

Boy, Kevin thought in disgust. *I really hate boy.*

"Boy!"

Kevin turned, smiling as nicely as he could. "Yes, ma'am?"

Kevin knew her but couldn't remember her name. . . . Trailer . . . Trainer . . . Traynor. That was it. Mrs. Traynor. Divorced, in her midforties, keeper of three raucous sons, ages six through eleven.

Ha, Kevin thought. *Jake is right. The more time you spend here, the more you find out about the guests and their families.*

"Boy," Mrs. Traynor said, her voice as sharp and icy as sleet. "I ordered eight towels over an hour ago. Where are my towels? I can't have my boys freezing when they come out of the pool dripping wet."

Freezing? Kevin thought in disbelief. *It's ninety degrees!*

What was worse, Kevin had lain out eight towels for Mrs. Traynor an hour earlier. In fact, he'd left them on the glass table next to her lounge chair—

They were gone.

Uh-oh.

"Well?" Mrs. Traynor growled. "Don't just stand there gaping. Get me the towels I asked for over an hour ago!"

17

Kevin smiled sheepishly. "Actually, I did get those towels earlier. They were right on that table. But someone must have swiped them. I'll get you more."

Mrs. Traynor's eyes narrowed. "Don't try to pass off your mistake by lying. There were never towels on that table. You ignored my order, and now you're trying to cover it up by suggesting that someone took the towels. Who would steal towels?"

Be nice, Kevin warned himself. *Be real, real nice.* He looked Mrs. Traynor directly in the eye. "Ma'am, if I make a mistake on the job, I'll be the first one to own up to it. But the towels were there. You don't have to insult me to get more. I'm always happy to get more towels."

Mrs. Traynor blinked in disbelief. "I can't believe this. Don't you talk back to me. You're the cabana boy, and I'm the guest. I pay your salary. In return, is it too much to ask that I get the towels I ordered over an hour ago? Is it too much to ask that this happen without debate?"

Kevin suddenly realized that he didn't even know if Austin Booth was around and overhearing the entire exchange. He could lose his job for talking back to a guest the way he just had. Who did Kevin think he was? Some rich kid who didn't need this gig? It was his *job* to be talked to that way by rude rich people.

Kevin was about to apologize and say he'd go get the towels when a pleasant voice cut him off.

"Of course not, Mrs. Traynor," the voice said. "I'm so sorry for the inconvenience. We'll get some towels for you right away."

Kevin turned to see a girl around his age dressed in the signature white polo shirt and shorts of the Surf City Resort Hotel. And man, she wore them well. She was gorgeous. Her dark hair was bobbed short just above her shoulders. Her blue eyes sparkled and met Kevin's.

"So go get the towels," she said in a perfectly normal voice.

Kevin gaped at her. *Who is she?* He'd never seen her before, and he thought he knew just about everyone who worked at the hotel by now.

"The towels?" she prodded, waving Kevin off.

He nodded, snapping himself out of it, and hustled to the towel bin near the rest-room shack. He snagged a huge stack of plush white towels with the hotel logo on them and delivered them to Mrs. Traynor.

The mystery girl was now talking to her and laughing. "Yes, I'm sorry for the mix-up, Mrs. Traynor. Sometimes people just grab any old towel. They aren't considerate at all."

"Thank you, Penny," Mrs. Traynor replied, her voice now as sweet as peach pie. "I certainly do appreciate it." She shot Kevin an icy glance. "Perhaps now I can get my sons ready for dinner. Boys!"

Mrs. Traynor moved off toward the pool to fetch her kids. Kevin stared after her, then dropped the towels on the table just like he'd done an hour earlier.

Then he noticed the mystery girl looking at him and smirking.

"Something funny?" Kevin asked.

The girl shrugged. "You're not cut out for this job,

are you?" she asked, her voice full of amusement.

Kevin bristled. "I just don't like being called a liar, even by a customer who's 'always right.'"

"Was she right?" the girl asked, cocking an eyebrow.

"Absolutely not," Kevin replied indignantly. "I dumped off those towels two minutes after she asked for them. It's not my fault someone else used them."

"That doesn't matter much to her, does it?" the girl said. "Your best bet around here is to just nod yes, move fast, and don't speak unless it's absolutely necessary."

Kevin huffed. "Servants should be seen and not heard, right?"

She smiled. "Now you're getting the hang of it."

"If that's true," Kevin pressed, "then how come she was so nice to you?"

The girl began walking away. Kevin walked with her, casually admiring her smooth, tan legs—while trying not to be obvious about it.

Nice stems, he thought.

"She was nice to me because you were about to give her an argument," the girl said, clearing an abandoned drink glass from a table and taking it with her. "When a situation gets to that point, all a guest wants is someone *else*. I knew you were in trouble the moment Mrs. Traynor called you over. I just waited for the right time to step in and save you."

Kevin smiled. "So you were watching the whole time?"

She nodded. "It's what I do."

"You watch cabana boys and wait for them to screw up?"

"Something like that," she replied. She smoothly put the drink glass on the bar and continued strolling around the pool. "I'm sort of a freelance problem solver."

"So you work with Jake?" Kevin probed, stepping faster to keep up.

"Not exactly," she replied.

"Who do you work for?"

Penny turned around and pointed at the resort's logo on her polo shirt, then turned back and resumed walking.

Kevin chuckled. "Duh. I meant—"

"I know what you meant," she said over her shoulder.

"So you're a manager? How's *that* possible?"

The girl stopped and turned to him. She glanced at the pool area for a moment, her eyes darting everywhere. "You don't think I could be a manager?"

Kevin resisted backing off a step. "You look like you're my age. I don't run into many fifteen-year-old managers around here."

The girl folded her arms across her chest. "I'm not a manager, but I'm management material."

Well, la-di-da, Kevin thought. The girl sure had confidence to burn. "So why haven't I seen you around here before?"

She tucked a strand of hair behind her ear. "I just got back yesterday from sleep-away camp in Arizona. My dad thought I should go for at least a month, even though I really wanted to work for the whole summer. I work here every summer; well, the past

21

two. That's how everyone knows me. So, are you gonna thank me for saving your butt or what?"

Kevin grinned. "Thank you for saving my butt."

The mystery girl nodded, satisfied. "Any other questions?"

"Yeah," Kevin said. "Two."

"Number one?"

"What's your name?" he asked.

She took a step back and pulled at her collar, then shifted her feet around. "Penny."

Kevin nodded, trying to interpret her body language. A challenge? A defense? No, she didn't seem the defensive type. "Mine's Kevin."

"I know," she replied. "What's the second question?"

"You know?" Kevin backtracked. *How did she know?*

"I know everyone's name who works here," she answered quickly. "It's my job. The second question?"

"Oh yeah, I forgot," Kevin said, holding up a finger as if he had a good idea. "Your nonmanagement management position."

"The second question?" she repeated with a smile.

"Second question, right . . . Why did you save my butt?"

Penny smiled. "Because you've never seen Mrs. Traynor get really angry. I have."

Kevin nodded. "Oh. I see. So it wasn't because . . ." His voice trailed off.

"What? Because I'm a nice person? Oh, you thought I was *flirting* with you. Is that it?" Penny's blue eyes challenged his. *Was she flirting, or was* she about to tell him to jump in the Pacific?

"You mean you don't like me?" he asked in mock devastation.

"I don't know you, Kevin," she replied. "I saved you because I'm a nice person—and because I take my job really seriously."

"But you know my name."

Penny smiled. "You should understand one thing about me. I operate under one rule: Make the guests happy at any cost. And I don't date coworkers, by the way."

Kevin met her gaze head-on. "So you're saying that if I asked you out, you'd pass?"

Penny smoothed her shiny hair. "That's right." She started walking away.

"Hey, Penny," Kevin called after her.

She stopped and turned around.

Could her eyes be any bluer? he wondered, mesmerized for a moment. "Um, just wanted to say thanks again. For saving my butt."

Penny nodded. "I guess there is one other thing you should know about me, Kevin."

"What's that?"

Her smile intensified. "I only save nice butts."

With that, she turned the corner and was gone. Kevin gaped after her, then shook his head and let out a deep breath.

Who was *that girl?*

An Excerpt from Penny's Diary

I met the cutest guy today. Kevin. A cabana boy. And I think he's a #3, Diary, I really do! To me, there are three kinds of guys. #1, objects of affection: the movie stars and lead singers you love from a distance (the Brad Pitts, the Leonardo DiCaprios, etc). #2, objects of avoidance: the really popular guys in school, like most of the baseball team, who are jerks under their amazingly cute faces and fake charm. Also in this category are the boarding-school types who wear cologne (ew!) and eat weird sushi (the nouveau-riche morons Dad tries to push my way). And #3, objects of connection: the guys who immediately speak to your heart and soul through words, actions, or smile.

There's no such thing as the perfect guy, but #3 is as perfect as a guy gets. They don't grow on trees, unfortunately. Or beaches.

But I might have met one today. Yeah. I think maybe I did. He certainly connected with me on the words-and-smile end. But before I get too excited, let's see how he does with the actions part. . . .

Did I mention his name is Kevin? I love that name.

Three

THE VOLLEYBALL SEEMED to float in slow motion above him. The evening sun reflected off the white of the ball, turning it amber, making the whole beach a strange desert world of color and shadow.

Kevin knew there was no more perfect sight in all of sports: the volleyball spinning in midair, descending toward him. Everything perfect . . . the angle . . . the set . . . the timing. It was a moment that could be captured in time, but not on paper.

Perhaps almost as much, Kevin loved the feel of a volleyball on his fingers. It had different textures, depending on what was happening: the hearty sting of a blocked spike, the sandpapery friction as he spun it in his palm, the warm, leathery spring when he pushed his fingers into it. You had your baseballs, your footballs, your basketballs, but no ball in all of sports begged to be slapped around more than the volleyball.

Kevin had drawn volleyballs a thousand times, but he could never get it right. He always found himself reduced to adding little comic-book flourishes to suggest movement. Little lines following the ball or making the ball oval. None of his efforts ever came close to a realistic picture of a volleyball in flight. It drove him mad sometimes.

Why was it so important for him to do that? V-ball was Kevin's second-favorite thing to do in life other than drawing. It made sense that he would want to capture his passions on paper. It just wasn't that easy for him sometimes. Not as easy, at least, as all the other stuff he could draw almost without looking at it.

"Slam it!"

Kevin leaped up at the net, timing the spike perfectly. He reared back, lashed out, and pounded the ball toward the sand on the other side of the net—

Johnny's hands blocked him. The ball careened back over to Kevin's side of the net and dropped to the sand.

"Stuffed!" Danny jeered, pointing at him.

Kevin crouched in the sand, glaring. The Ford brothers had been practicing for over an hour, trying to get in as much work as possible before dark. And that was the third time Johnny had blocked one of his spikes. It was getting tedious. As was Danny's trash talk.

"Stuffed like a Pooh bear! Stuffed like the Thanksgiving turkey! Stuffed like the Christmas goose! Stuffed like a training bra—"

Kevin shot Danny a death stare. "Your mouth is

gonna be stuffed with my sweat socks if you don't stuff it first."

"Ooooooooh," Danny taunted. "You've been watching too much violence on TV."

"Dude," Johnny said, bending under the net and offering his hand to Kevin, "you have to get up higher and snap quicker. I'm reading your eyes. I know right where you're hitting it."

He took Johnny's helping hand and stood, then brushed sand off his Dave Matthews Band T-shirt. "That's funny. I thought my eyes were closed."

"I'm not trying to be a jerk, Kev," Johnny commented. "But you're the shortest of all three of us. Everyone in that tournament will be pounding around me to spike at you. Be ready for it."

"How do you know that?" Kevin asked.

"Because that's what I'd do," Johnny replied, shrugging. "It's not your vertical leap, dude. It's your hands. You're not being fast enough up over the net."

"But you're going to be doing all the spiking, Johnny," Kevin protested. "That's always been the deal: Danny serves, I set, you spike."

Johnny laughed. "Are you kidding? This tournament isn't a pickup game at Spring Valley High. These guys will cut us apart into our weakest elements. Sure, I'll do most of the spiking, but I won't always be able to. We have to do it all and be it all. Or we're dead."

They worked on more spikes and blocks. Kevin grew more and more frustrated. He simply wasn't tall enough. He'd turned fifteen last month, but he was still a couple of years away from his true height. Johnny was a half foot taller and worked him over like a junior leaguer.

"C'mon, Kev," Johnny urged, "get torqued."

Yeah. Johnny knew his brother, all right. The angrier Kevin got, the more focused he got. He'd always been like that. Rage threw most guys right off their games. But not Kevin.

On the far side of the net Danny bumped the ball into the air for Johnny to spike it. Kevin watched . . . waited . . . timed.

. . . you're the shortest . . .

The ball peaked, pausing in midair.

. . . everyone will be pounding around me to spike at you . . .

Kevin tensed as the ball hurtled toward him.

. . . get torqued!

He went for the net. Johnny went up with him, anticipating. Kevin ignored him, focusing on the ball. His hand snapped out like the head of a striking snake. Kevin's eyes rolled left. Johnny's body instinctively followed.

But Kevin spiked right.

The ball rocketed into the sand four feet from a diving Danny. Johnny came down on the sand away from the play. He spit grains from his lips and started laughing.

"Ooooooooh!" Kevin catcalled, stomping over to Danny's prone form. "Who got stuffed? But not just stuffed. Stuffed and *mounted!* You're on my wall,

28

sucker! Horns and all, on my wall!" Kevin did a touch-down dance. "Horns and all, on my wall, horns and all, on my wall!" Then he made as if he were holding a drink, taking on a snooty, first-class voice. "Mmm, yes, that's the pale-faced, jobless loudmouth sloth. I call him Danny. A fine specimen, don't you think? I shot that particular specimen on my hunt to Tangiers, you know. That was back in 2000. Bad year for waterfowl. But the sloth population was all the rage. This little bugger kept taunting me from the underbrush. Just couldn't keep his mouth shut. So I bagged him and stuffed him, one shot, no waiting. Yes, yes, I know, I am great. Tell me again if you like, but I do know it. No, go ahead, tell me again. G-r-e-a-t. Don't be shy."

"Oh, shut up." Danny moaned, throwing the volleyball at Kevin.

The ball bounced off his head—*doink*—straight into the air. Kevin only smiled at his brothers. "Have I proved myself yet?"

Johnny chuckled. "Maybe for today. But tomorrow's another day."

Danny retrieved the ball. "We done or what?"

Johnny nodded. "Yeah, we're done. What's for dinner?"

"There's ramen noodles in the kitchen," Kevin offered. "And extra cheese on the inside of last night's pizza box, which I forgot to throw out. Gourmet all around."

"What flavor noodles?" Danny asked.

"Pork, pork, and pork," Kevin replied, counting them off on his fingers.

"Sounds like Kevin's tip money is buying dinner again," Johnny declared, slapping his younger brother on the shoulder.

Kevin brushed Johnny's hand away, a wave of disgruntled anger flowing through him. This would be the fourth time in two weeks that he had to use his tip money to buy dinner for the brothers. His wages were contributed to the collective cause (rent, etc.), but his tip money was supposed to be his own. It was all because Danny had lost his job. And it was all totally unfair.

"Great, yet another day's tips sucked up by the almighty sponge," Kevin grumbled, glaring at Danny.

"Temporary, dude," Danny assured him. "Totally temporary. It's tough finding a summer job this deep into the summer. But Raven's making sure I pound the pavement every day."

"What a sweetheart," Johnny replied, rolling his eyes. "Must be hard filling out a job application when you're riding a skateboard up and down the boardwalk."

"At least I get to ride a skateboard with an actual girl," Danny shot back, spinning the volleyball on his finger for emphasis. "Can any of you lameoid social outcasts say the same?"

Kevin immediately thought of Penny. He didn't know why—it's not like they were dating or anything. Sure, she was hot. Sure, she seemed to flirt with him. And sure, he had been thinking about her since he met her that afternoon. But that didn't exactly erase an entire summer of being a lameoid social outcast.

But those beautiful blue eyes, those tan legs. Yeah, he'd been thinking quite a bit about her.

"I met someone," he said, before he even realized it.

"What?" Danny asked. "A girl?"

Kevin smirked. "Yeah, a girl. At work."

"Oh no." Johnny moaned, shaking his head. "Here we go again."

"What?" Kevin asked.

"You've got that same stupid, goofy look in your eye that Danny had when he met Raven," Johnny declared. "And you know how that turned out."

Danny shrugged. "I thought it turned out rather well, myself."

Johnny held up a stern finger. "No way. Not again. I am not going through that nonsense. We are here to play volleyball, and we finally have our game up to a respectable level, thanks in no small part to the three of us having no lives whatsoever. And that's the way I like it."

Danny let out a long laugh. "Losers at love, winners at play."

"Sounds like an episode of Leeza," Kevin replied.

Johnny shook his head. "I'm serious. Except for Mr. Unemployment here, we've lived in peace and harmony for a couple of weeks. Life is good. I want to keep it that way."

"Speak for yourself, you monk," Kevin countered.

"At least you get to rescue a rich daughter in a bikini now and then. All I do is schlep towels and take abuse. I mean, other than what it says on the calendar, this isn't a summer for me. It stinks. And I'm not going to jump down a manhole every time a girl talks to me just because my older brother thinks it will mess with the grand scheme of things. And by the way, this girl and I barely even spoke. We just *met*. You know, the process in which pleasantries and names are exchanged in a sterile environment. You act like I cut off my ring finger so she could wear it around her neck."

"Ouch," Danny said. "That's harsh. All Raven wanted was my soul in a little jar."

"All right, all right," Johnny relented, hands up in surrender. "I get the point. I just want you guys to see the big picture."

"Dude, I painted the big picture," Kevin replied. "I'll be out on this court every night, just like always. Even if she *did* say I have a nice butt."

Danny howled with laughter. "I knew it. I knew there was something else there. You call that exchanging pleasantries in a sterile environment?"

Kevin grinned. "I shower."

"So who is this mystery woman?" Johnny demanded. "Do I know her?"

Kevin shrugged. "I don't know. Maybe you've seen her around the pool. She's got brown hair, blue eyes, and hot legs and looks great in white hotel shorts."

"Except for the blue eyes, you just described

32

yourself," Danny remarked, bouncing the ball off Kevin's head again.

Kevin shoved him. "What do you want, a composite drawing? She's hot, trust me."

"Point her out to me tomorrow," Johnny suggested. "Then we'll get a read on just what kind of girl would think you have a nice butt."

"Hey, your brother just said I have hot legs," Kevin replied goofily. "What do you want from my life?"

A loud voice coming from the beach made them pause. "Yo! Check it out. It's a used-Ford dealership!"

The brothers turned. Kevin spotted three figures walking toward them out of the sunset. The silhouettes were tall and muscular. Shaggy, long hair. Very familiar.

A burst of adrenaline flooded Kevin.

It was Tanner St. John. He stood six-four, with the usual world-class volleyballer body: lean and muscular. His overtanned volleyball cronies were with him: Arliss Neeson, a thick dude with a protruding lantern jaw and bushy black eyebrows over dark eyes, and Shooter Ridge, a cologne-smelling specimen whose dark hair was always molded with gel.

True to their names and haircuts, Tanner and his buds were about as appealing as a glue sandwich. Obnoxious, overbearing bullies. And the worst part? They could back it all up with action.

These are the kind of guys who could only happen in southern California, Kevin thought.

But Kevin also knew just how good those guys were at volleyball. Tanner was an all-American at California University, and all three had helped that team win the national championship. But even more immediate, the Ford brothers had played these guys in an "unofficial" three-on-three beach game a month earlier. Danny had just met Raven and was in his useless phase. But that didn't excuse the beating the Fords took at the hands of the national champs: twenty-one to one.

Kevin had never been involved in such a humiliating defeat. It tore a rift in the brothers—at first. But then it brought them together and showed them just what they were getting into with the tournament.

Tanner and his buds were the team to beat.

And Kevin wasn't sure if the Fords could do it.

"Saw you practicing, kids," Tanner said, hands on hips. "And I must say that I was very impressed. Especially with you, squirt." He nodded at Kevin. "It took you all night, but you finally got your stubby little hand over that nasty old net."

"Squirt this," Kevin replied.

Tanner only laughed. "Very clever, young grasshopper. You want to back up that so very tough talk with some action? Say, ten bucks a point to twenty-one?"

"We'll even spot you twenty points," Shooter added with a laugh. "That should at least make a game of it."

Shooter and Arliss grinned and high-fived.

"If we're so lousy," Johnny challenged, "why were you watching us practice for the last hour?"

Tanner just smiled. "We were just waiting for you to finish. We didn't want to practice on the court next to you. You might have found it intimidating. And it was so sweet the way you were bipping the ball around to each other. I wish I had a camera to send a picture home to Mom."

"Why? Does your mom like teenage boys?" Kevin asked. He heard Johnny sigh and Danny suppress a guffaw.

Tanner's face darkened. "I meant *your* mom, stupid."

Kevin shrugged. "What do I know? I'm just a dumb kid."

"So what do you say, little Fords?" Shooter asked, flipping a ball in his hands. "Do we have a game?"

Kevin eyed his brothers. He could tell that Danny was up for it. But Johnny? Not a chance. The oldest Ford brother just stood there with an amused look on his face, arms folded, shaking his head.

"No thanks, champs," Johnny replied. "We work for a living. Which means when practice is over, we're outta here."

Tanner snickered. "Oh yeah. I forgot. You pull old ladies out of the surf over at the hotel. And you," he added, pointing at Kevin, "are the famous towel boy of Surf City. Word on the street says you can get a towel for anyone, anytime, anyplace. Is that true? Would you get me a towel now?"

Kevin never felt his blood boil, but right then he couldn't be sure. His face was hot as a griddle, and his eyes locked on Tanner's for what seemed like an eternity. Normally a guy like Tanner wouldn't bother Kevin. But when it came to his job, Kevin knew he was lower than low. And he hated it.

"I can get you that towel, Tan," Kevin replied, his voice icy and even. "But you'll have to figure out what to do with it all by yourself."

"Such a dangerous wit from such a little dude," Tanner retorted, casually flexing. Then he grew serious. "Watch that mouth, kid, or you'll find your leg being used as a toothpick."

Johnny stepped forward. "We've blown enough smoke for one night. We're outta here."

Johnny herded his brothers toward the boardwalk and home. It was all Kevin could do not to turn around and stare at the team to beat, their archenemies.

"See you at the tournament, scumbags," Tanner called. "We'll bring a mop for the bloodbath."

That did it. Kevin couldn't resist a look over his shoulder—coupled with a discreet but emphatic hand gesture. Sure, it was a childish thing to do, but since everyone kept reminding him how small he was, it seemed appropriate. Bottom line? One thing burned Kevin more than the catcalls and trash talk: the fact that deep down, he didn't know if he could spike one past Tanner St. John. If the Fords could really beat those guys.

That fear really got Kevin *torqued*.

Four

T HE NEXT DAY at work Kevin was bent over, clearing several drink glasses from a side table onto a tray, when two smooth, tan legs came into view. They were attached to immaculate white canvas sneakers and athletic socks.

One foot was tapping impatiently.

Kevin slowly straightened and stared at her. Penny was so beautiful! Stunning blue eyes, gorgeous face, amused smile. Today her silky brown hair was pulled back.

"What did I do now?" Kevin asked in mock exhaustion. She was definitely flirting with him. The foot tapping had to be a flirtatious gesture. Right?

"If you think you did something wrong," Penny said, "then you probably did. Apologize so we can get on with our lives."

Kevin smiled. "So sorry."

She laughed. "That's better. Don't let it happen again."

Kevin nodded and continued clearing the glasses. "To what do I owe this honor? Is someone short some towels? I'm really good with towels."

Penny folded her arms and regarded him. "Sarcasm suits you, you know. No, no one is short any towels. At least not right now. But from the sound of your voice, you're a guy who doesn't really like his job, aren't you?"

Kevin stood up, shot her a grin, and gestured grandly at the pool area. "Oh, I don't know. I mean, look around. Isn't this a fun place?"

"You could do a lot worse," Penny reminded him. "You could be peddling ice cream up and down the boardwalk. How about frying burgers?"

Kevin raised an eyebrow. "What's the difference? A job's a job, right? Hey, you're not gonna get me in trouble with Jake, are you?"

She smiled a dazzling white smile. "No way. I'm just acting in my capacity here at the hotel as universal problem solver. I'm supposed to make sure the employees are happy. Or at least marginally happy. When you're happy, you make the guests happy, which makes the boss happy. Which, again, should make you happy. It's one big circle."

"A vicious circle," Kevin muttered.

"Hey, you *should* be happy," Penny said seriously. "You could be doing so much worse. At least this place is luxurious. Why not work at a gorgeous hotel that has everything you could possibly want, including

38

wealthy patrons who tip well? You could be out there delivering pizza to some cheapo who won't tip you a quarter. Or who will try to rip you off."

Kevin grabbed the last of the glasses and moved toward the bar to drop them off. Penny moved with him. "I don't know from pizza deliverymen. But bump up my base pay a couple of bucks an hour, and we'll start to talk tolerance. Happiness? Never. Tolerance? Maybe. But not at my bargain wages."

"You could always quit," Penny suggested.

Kevin shot her an absurd glance. "Quitting is not an option. Not when you have two brothers depending on your third for food and shelter. No, I'm what is known as an involuntary, obligated doofus."

Penny laughed and snatched the tray away from him. "Good. I'm glad you've decided to stay. It would be less scenic around here without you."

A wave of heat flowed through Kevin. Whoa. Did she mean that as an offhand comment . . . or something more? *Oh, come on,* he told himself. *Listen to the girl. She just told you that she likes looking at you. Remember your butt?*

Play it cool, dude, he warned himself. *Don't say something stupid. Don't let her know she has you rattled. Ha! Rattled? I am Joe Cool/Brad Pitt/Puffy Combs cool.*

Penny marched to the bar and deposited the empties, brushing her hands clean. "There. I hope I've made your job a little easier and your day a little brighter. Now I'll move on to someone else who's short on the sunshine."

Penny brushed past him with a sly smile. Kevin

knew full well how to play this particular game. He just wasn't sure he was supposed to. Not in broad daylight in front of a crowded pool full of guests who desperately needed his towel-bearing services. But he couldn't let her get away. Not now.

"You always do people's jobs for them?" he asked.

Penny halted and turned. "Only those who are so obviously desperate."

She glanced around the pool area, then gave him her attention again. Who was she constantly looking for? he wondered. Guests who needed something? A jealous boyfriend? Her boss? Kevin peered around. He didn't see Jake anywhere. It was Kevin's turn to smile. "I look desperate?"

She grinned. "*You* told me so yourself, not thirty seconds ago."

"I never said anything about desperate," Kevin replied.

Penny took a step toward him. "Maybe you know how to put up a bold front."

Kevin stepped forward himself, undaunted. "Maybe I'm just a good liar."

She tapped a thoughtful finger against her chin, nodding. "Either way, Kevin, you're exactly what the hotel looks for in a towel mule."

"Desperate liars," Kevin replied, crossing his arms. "I'm starting to wonder if I should be offended."

Penny laughed and spun on her heel. "If you have to wonder," she called over her shoulder, "then you're hopeless too."

Kevin watched her walk away. He had just

participated in the Flirt. No. The Major Flirt. The back-and-forthing, the one-upping, the ever so slight jabbing. She liked him. She had to. Otherwise why would Ms. Manager waste her beloved guests' time yakking it up with him?

She liked him. Now all he had to do was ask her out, and his summer was set.

Penny would make a much more interesting subject to draw than another killer wave.

Several hours passed. Kevin thought a lot about Penny but didn't see much of her. A glimpse here and there. She truly did wander the hotel all day, doing everything under the sun. Not bad work if you could get it, he figured.

He took his afternoon break at the far end of the big bar, which was built into a large, fake-grass-topped hut. He sipped his complimentary bottle of spring water and tried to flex some of the stiffness out of his knees and feet.

He slipped his hand in his pocket and felt the crumpled wad of the day's tips. Not bad. As long as his brothers didn't decide that he was paying for pizza once again that night. Man, that Danny *had* to find a job soon. Let *him* flip some burgers.

Kevin resisted the urge to pull out his tip money and count it. *Never count your money when you're sitting at the table,* the wise man once said. *There'll be time enough for counting when the towel dealing's done.*

"Hey, hopeless," came a familiar voice. "Want to make two dollars the hard way?"

"Is there any other way?" Kevin immediately replied.

Penny slipped onto the bar stool next to him. Kevin sipped his water and smiled, that magical warmth filling him once again. He didn't want to admit it, but he was beginning to enjoy Penny's little flirtations.

"Has your day improved?" Penny asked, resting her head on her hand.

Kevin's grin widened. "Just now."

Penny smiled back. A shy smile, he noticed. And was that a little hint of red he saw on her creamy cheeks? "Well, my work here is finished. I guess I can go home for the day."

She slipped off the bar stool and turned to go.

"Hey, wait a minute," Kevin called.

Penny turned back.

"I was just wondering . . ." Kevin grabbed his water bottle, climbed off his stool, and approached her.

"Wondering what?" she asked, her head slightly tilted.

"Is it always so easy for you?"

Penny blinked, taken aback. "What do you mean?"

Kevin gestured at the entire scene surrounding them. "This. All of this. You act like you own the place. It's easy for you. And how you came up to me earlier. That was easy too. So I was just wondering. Is it always so easy for you?"

"Maybe I just try hard to make it *look* easy," she said. "I'm not one of those people who pulls an attitude the second something goes wrong or I don't get my way."

"Yeah, but you must get tired of all the stupid stuff. The Mrs. Traynors, people like that."

"Of course I do," she said. "But when I look around here, I don't see whining, complaining guests who scream if their coffee isn't light enough. I see beautiful grounds, a huge, blue, clean swimming pool, tons of trees and flowers, and an amazing beach just down there. I feel sort of privileged to work here."

"Yeah, but—"

"Yeah, but nothing, Kevin. I don't really get what there is to complain about. It's summer; I get to work outdoors most of the time; I have an entire beach to hang out on. What's so bad? So yeah, maybe it is easy for me. Because *I* make it easy."

"It's summer for me too, and I get to work outdoors too, and nothing is easy for me," Kevin remarked. "You must have a secret trick for not being a whiner."

Penny smiled. "Anything too easy isn't much fun. I *like* to work hard. I work hard at school. I work hard at work. I work hard on this tan." She laughed. "You know what I mean, right?"

Kevin grinned a charming grin. "I do indeed. And since you like things on the not-so-easy side, maybe you'd be interested in complicating things further for yourself."

"Complicating things?" she echoed. "In what way, exactly?"

He cleared his throat and tried to forget all the people splashing and sunning around them. "By adding some romance to your life. What I mean is, would you like to go out with me? You know, sometime?"

He caught the smile before she could hide the fact that she was flattered. Good. That meant he hadn't been wrong. She did like him.

Penny eyed him, then her gaze flicked away for a split second. What was in that split second? A bit of sudden shyness at getting asked out? Or a complete vision of their first date: a romantic disaster of *Titanic* proportions, wreckage, twisted metal, no good-night kiss.

Or did she see something good?

"What do you say, Penny?" Kevin asked again. "Would you like to go out sometime?"

Penny glanced down. She seemed uncomfortable. "No."

Kevin blinked, his face frozen in a smiling mask.

No?

Huh?

But—

No.

Talk about humiliating.

"No," he repeated.

Penny shook her head. "Sorry, Kevin. I am flattered, though."

Kevin managed to get some of his motor skills back and nodded. "I see. Okay. Cool. Just wanted to check with you first."

"I don't date coworkers, Kevin," she announced. "I told you that. It's a good policy. It keeps things—"

"Nice and difficult, the way you like. 'Cause that way you're attracted to someone, you like them, but you can't go out with them."

Penny looked at the floor. "I said it's my policy."

"Okay, then. You're busy. I'll just get back to my towels." Kevin turned to go, sure that his face was as red as the surface of Mars.

"Kevin?" Penny called.

He paused. "Yeah?"

She sidled up next to him. He noticed that her fists were clenching and unclenching at her sides. "Um, now that I've given you the textbook answer that I give any amorous coworkers, I just wanted to say that if you decided for some reason to wander around the amusement pier tonight around eight, and if I happened to be there, and if we happened to hang out, well, then it wouldn't really be two coworkers on a date, would it? It would just be two coworkers bumping into each other by chance."

Kevin nodded, excitement growing inside him. "Stopping to chat."

"Having a soda," Penny added.

"Being cordial and polite."

"Engaging in small talk."

"Exactly," Kevin said confidently. "No one could possibly complain about that, could they?"

"That is," Penny continued, "if you actually wandered by the amusement pier and I happened to be there at that time."

"Hypothetically," Kevin replied.

"Totally hypothetically," Penny agreed.

They stared at each other for a beat. Kevin's heart was racing. This was the coolest date acceptance he'd ever gotten. Considering that theoretically he had been, in fact, shot down in flames.

"So I guess it's possible we could bump into each other tonight," Kevin concluded.

Penny shrugged. "I dunno."

"Me either," Kevin replied.

This made Penny smile. "Well, Kevin. Have a great rest of the day. I have to return to my duties, and so do you. We've had quite enough chitchat."

"Small talk."

"That too."

Kevin nodded. "You have a great day too. Maybe I'll see you around somewhere, you know, random."

Penny gave him a little wink and a smile. "Maybe you will."

"Dude, you can't bother me right now," Johnny said. "I'm supposed to be keeping a count here." The eldest Ford leaned against his lifeguard chair, casually tapping the little bright orange *Baywatch* floater that went wherever he went while on duty. And on duty was exactly what Johnny was at the moment.

"You gotta be kidding, bro," Kevin replied, impatiently gesturing at the surf. "It's four in the afternoon. There're three people in the water, and they

46

all have surfboards! Who's going to drown?"

Johnny shook his head and continued staring out at the ocean. "Did you want something?"

"You and Danny are on your own for dinner tonight," Kevin told him. "I have plans."

"Oh yeah?"

Kevin inflated with pride. "I have a date."

"Well, well, well," Johnny said. "Way to go, little bro. How ugly is she?"

An image of Penny floated through Kevin's mind. Those eyes. That pretty hair. Those tanned legs. That adorable mouth. "She's totally hot. I told you."

"Oh, that's right. That goddess of a girl who works here," Johnny recalled, nodding. "Describe her again? Maybe I've noticed her."

"Medium-length brown, straight hair, blue eyes, long, tan legs—"

"Wait a minute!" Johnny exclaimed, snapping his fingers. "I know who you mean. Cute girl, about yay-high. Always walking around with a clipboard. Kind of has a Rachael Leigh Cook thing going?"

"That's her," Kevin said with a quick nod. "Hot, right?"

"What's her name again?"

"Penny."

He started to laugh. "Penny what?"

Kevin blinked. He realized he had no idea what Penny's last name was. It didn't really matter, though. Not now anyway. There was plenty of time for names later. Like tonight, for example. "I don't know. Who cares? She wants to go out with me."

Johnny laughed even harder. "I know what her last name is, dude."

"You do?" Kevin asked urgently. "What is it? And what's so funny?"

"Booth," Johnny said, turning to face him. "Penny's last name is *Booth*."

Kevin nodded. "Okay. Booth. Penny Booth. How did you know—"

A bolt of realization shot through Kevin, freezing him to the spot. Johnny saw the look on his face and broke into mad gales of laughter. "Yes, Kevin . . . you hit the jackpot. Penny Booth! As in Austin Booth!"

"Austin Booth," Kevin mumbled distantly.

"That's right, Kevin," Johnny announced. "You're dating the boss's daughter!"

Instant-Messaging Transcript

Penny15: So what should I do? Keep the date with Kevin or cancel?

JenniferT: Cancel! Just use your excuse: no dating coworkers. He'll buy that. No hurt feelings. And that's the point, Penny: No one's feelings get hurt.

Penny15: But it's different this time. I *really* like Kevin.

JenniferT: I'm your best friend, remember? You can't fool me. You're only interested in him because he's "forbidden" by your dad.

Penny15: No, it's not like that. Kevin and I really click. I feel like I can talk to him, *really* talk to him. There's something different about him.

JenniferT: Uh-huh. Right. That's why you haven't told him you're the big boss's daughter! Look, Penny, I know you wish your dad paid more attention to you, especially with your mom away in Europe for the summer. I know that's why you work so hard at the hotel. But dating a forbidden guy just to get your dad's attention isn't fair.

Penny15: That's not why I'm interested in Kevin. Maybe I flirted with him at first because of that. But the more I got to know him, the more I liked him. And now I can't get him out of my mind.

JenniferT: Wow, so you really like this guy. Wait a minute. Are you crazy? Kevin's a cabana boy. Your father is going to kill you!

Five

KEVIN LOVED THE boardwalk at night. The whole town came alive in surging yellow and red light; loud, incongruous blasts of different music; and the pungent smells of sawdust, cheap perfume, and greasy french fries.

People were everywhere. Children of all shapes, sizes, and colors, their faces pink with dried cotton candy. Through it all came the sounds of roller-coaster screams, balloons popping, winning buzzers sounding, and carousel music.

Yeah, the boardwalk was pretty cool. You saw all kinds. Kevin wished he could take a break on a bench with his sketch pad—try to capture some of what he was seeing—but it was nearly eight o'clock. It was time to see if Penny was serious about "bumping into him."

Johnny had, of course, ridden him about her all the way home after work. And he had, of course, told Danny about it as soon as they got home. So Kevin took brotherly abuse from two sides. Most of it was the good-natured abuse that was really a guy's way of congratulating another guy. But Kevin also heard the undertones in Johnny's comments: *Be careful, bro—she's still the boss's daughter, and this could blow up in your face.*

Ah, Johnny Ford's patented lecture series, volume two, episode twelve.

Yeah, it could blow up, Kevin thought. *But the world could blow up in all our faces at any time, so what's the point of being scared?*

And Penny seemed genuinely interested, especially when Kevin stripped away all her flirtations and smoke screen and simply looked into her eyes. The eyes never lied, and her eyes told him that she would indeed "bump into him" at the amusement pier tonight.

Yet a flicker of doubt jumped in his brain too. *What if she doesn't show?*

Then Kevin was going to pump thirty bucks into Skee-Ball and win the cheesiest, cheapest plastic prize he could. Then he'd take it home and burn it.

But that wasn't going to happen. She'd show. Kevin could feel it. The butterflies in his stomach proved it.

By eight-fifteen, however, Kevin wasn't so sure. He'd slowly made his way up and down the amusement pier twice. Up past the weight-and-age guessers, the psychics, and the Rumblegrudge roller coaster (three loops and a corkscrew!). Down past

Howie's House o' Haunts, the carousel, and the games of chance (bust a balloon, win a baboon!). Kevin saw a lot of cute girls with long, brown hair and tan legs. But no Penny.

Bummer, he thought glumly. *Major bummer.*

Then he reminded himself: *It's a big pier.* She could be at the opposite end, looking for him that very moment. Man, why didn't they just agree on a place to meet? It would've been so much easier. Ah, but then that would've been a deliberately planned date, which was illegal. It had to be a random encounter. A carefully planned accident of boy meeting girl, boy treating girl, and girl being so impressed that she can no longer live without boy. Right?

Riiiiighht.

But first boy had to meet girl.

Kevin stopped at a concession stand and bought a Fizz Cola. Then he wandered over to the Strongman setup to watch the muscle-bound morons pound the hammer to ring the bell. Two big football-playing dudes tried to outdo the other and impress their girlfriends by slamming the hammer as hard as they could. But no dice: The little weight came within about a foot of the bell, but no dinger.

Kevin had read about this game somewhere. It didn't matter how strong you were. It mattered where you hit the lever with the hammer. It was all physics. First of all, the widest arc produced the greatest hammer speed. So you had to extend. If you had long arms, so much the better. Then you had to hit the lever as far away from the weight as possible to create the most spring.

The two football dudes didn't look like they went to many physics classes.

"It's not how strong you are," came a voice. "It's where you hit it."

His mouth open, Kevin turned to see Penny. Not only had she shown up after all, but the girl obviously read the same stuff he did.

The butterflies instantly took flight once again. She looked great in her shorts and cotton tank top. Her hair was pulled back like it had been earlier, but some tendrils had escaped. She had on a pretty gold ring with a pearl centered around some stones he couldn't make out. A gold watch, brand unknown. And down at the bottom of those beautiful tan legs? A gold ankle bracelet.

Kevin was no expert, but the stuff looked expensive. And why not? The girl was rich, after all.

Why did Kevin suddenly feel nervous?

"Hi," he said with a grin. Then he looked around comically. "Wow, Penny, imagine seeing you here!"

She laughed. "Yeah, that is so weird. What a coincidence! I should spend more time on the boardwalk. You never know who you'll run into."

"It's amazing," Kevin gushed. "Isn't it amazing? I'm amazed."

"Okay, okay, I think we killed that dead horse," she said with a chuckle. Her eyes sparkled as she gazed at him. "So what do we do now?"

Kevin smiled sheepishly and shrugged. "I don't know. What do you want to do?"

She glanced at the hammer-slamming game. "I want to see you ring the bell."

Kevin smiled. "You're right, you know. It isn't how strong you are. It's knowing where to hit the hammer."

Penny flashed a devilish smile. "Are you agreeing with me because you don't think you can do it?"

Kevin's eyebrows arched. "Maybe I'm agreeing with you because you're the boss's daughter."

Penny stared at him for a moment. "So you figured it out." Her eyes narrowed suspiciously. "Or did you know all along?"

Kevin shook his head. "I didn't know at all. My brother told me."

"Oh yeah, the lifeguard. Johnny, right?"

"Right. Anyway, I didn't know that your true identity was such a secret."

Penny shrugged. "It's not, I guess. I mean, most of the guests know me because they know my father. And I don't want people thinking I'm spying on them or something. It shouldn't make a difference who I am." She paused. "Is it a problem now that you know?"

"I wouldn't have shown up if it was a problem." Kevin offered her a sip of his soda. As she drank, he added, "But it does explain a few things."

Penny licked her lips, handed him back the cup, and began walking toward the ocean end of the pier. "Such as?"

Kevin settled in beside her, enjoying the closeness. They walked slowly, swaying back and forth and occasionally bumping. The skin of her arm felt warm against his own. "Well, let's see. It explains why you float around doing everything under the sun at the hotel. It explains why it's so easy for you to talk to the guests."

Penny smiled knowingly. "You think my job is a joke, Kevin? A gift from Daddy for the summer?"

Kevin shook his head, wondering how to get his feet out of the sticky mess he'd just stepped in. "I didn't say that, Penny. We're just talking here. Getting to know each other."

"I know," she replied with a sigh. "I just couldn't bear sitting around a pool all summer, doing my nails. I see girls my age doing it every day at that hotel. But I like to work. I want to work."

"Even though you don't have to?" Kevin probed.

"Even though I don't have to," Penny confirmed.

"Wow," Kevin replied. "I've never had a choice. I don't know what I'd do if I did have one. I think I'd have to use the time to draw."

Penny smiled. "You draw?"

"Whenever I can. I just wish I had more time." Kevin allowed himself to imagine for a moment. "Man, if I didn't have to work, I'd really try to create something special. A mural, a painting, something. I could spend hours and hours on it. All day, all night. Take breaks just to eat." Kevin stared up at the sky for a moment. "Doesn't that sound amazing? I could spend my time *my* way instead of the *necessary* way."

Penny playfully yanked the soda cup from Kevin and sipped from the straw. "What do you draw?"

"Everything," he replied. "Anything. Whatever happens to catch my eye at the time."

Penny cocked a flirtatious eyebrow. "Would you draw me?"

Kevin pretended to think about it, furrowing his brow and looking skyward again. "Well . . . I dunno. You'd have to catch my eye first."

Penny laughed. "You mean I haven't caught your eye yet?"

Kevin played it mock cool. "Well, you know, I just came out here because you seemed so desperate. You don't have all that much going for you. I didn't want you to have to face yet another disappointment."

Penny slumped her shoulders and offered a pathetic expression. "My secret's out. I'm really a loser. Thank you, oh, thank you, Kevin Ford, for taking pity on me. Thank you for desperately asking me out today. Thank you for chasing me halfway across the hotel patio to catch me to ask me to go on a date with you. Where would I be without you?"

"Probably polishing your nails," Kevin replied with a grin.

"So we agree," Penny said seriously.

"Agree?"

"Agree," she said again. "That it's not going to matter."

Okay, she'd lost him. He had no idea what she was talking about.

"That I'm Austin Booth's daughter," she clarified.

Ah. *That* little snag again. But Kevin knew it *wasn't* a snag. Just because Penny was the big head honcho's kid, just because her father had more money than anyone he could think of, just because he was the lowest man on the totem pole of Austin Booth's empire didn't mean that he and Penny couldn't make a go of their attraction.

And attracted they were. That was clear. And that was important point *numero uno*.

Second key thing was that they made each other laugh.

Third was that they *wanted* to be together.

So what did money have to do with anything? *Zilcherooo*. Except for the fact that she had lots, and he had none. Well, except for his own pathetic salary.

"We agree," he told her.

They didn't speak for a bit. They just walked along the pier, watching the passersby, watching the people on the rides, watching each other out of the corner of their eyes. Kevin finished the soda and tossed the cup in a trash barrel from three-point range. Penny seemed impressed. That was a good sign. If he couldn't impress her by taking her out for the best lobster in Surf City (which was probably in the restaurant of her dad's hotel, by the way), he needed to be able to impress her with his own skills and talents.

He wondered if she'd be impressed by his drawings. He hoped so.

She didn't come across as a rich girl. At least, not like the rich girls he saw around the hotel pool. The wealth shone through Penny in different ways. Her not-obnoxious-but-obviously-expensive accessories, for one. Her confidence, for another. There wasn't much hesitation in the girl, which Kevin understood to be a trait of the rich. Penny never seemed to waste time, whether she was attending to guests at the pool or flirting with Kevin.

But Kevin? He seemed to do nothing but waste time. He worked hard, but when it came time to be on his own, all he could do was grab a pen and doodle without much thought involved. And that was because work was so exhausting. Who had the energy to create something really great? His free time had to be for vegging out. Just the thought of knowing he had to be back at the grind tomorrow morning exhausted him even more.

"So," Penny said. "I have a suggestion for what we can do tonight."

Kevin squeezed her hand. "You do?"

"I do." She nodded.

"What?"

Penny's gaze slowly turned toward the neon archway blinking the word *Rumblegrudge*. She grinned at him. "You like roller coasters, Kevin?"

They walked through the rose-covered archway that led from the boardwalk into the hotel property. It was almost midnight. The moon had burst across the sky, bathing them in a milky silver glow and throwing deep shadows across the path. A light sea breeze blew through their hair,

59

cool, but not cold like summer nights can be.

Kevin couldn't believe what a great time he'd had.

He'd known he'd enjoy himself with Penny. But he didn't anticipate having the time of his life. They rode the roller coaster four times. They went through the haunted house twice. And yes, Kevin busted a balloon to win a baboon. But the last fun of the evening came as they made their way off the amusement pier. They stopped at the hammer-slammer bell-ringer stand. Finally Kevin caved to Penny's taunts and decided to test all those theories of physics he'd heard about.

They were true indeed. He rang the bell two out of three times, making all the muscle men stare at him in awe.

Then they walked back to the hotel in the moonlight, Kevin licking some cotton candy, Penny cradling her stuffed baboon.

"Are you gonna get in trouble for being out this late?" Kevin asked.

"Trouble?" Penny turned to him and tilted her head. "What do you mean?"

He stared at her for a second. "I mean, from your dad."

Penny laughed. "Are you kidding? My dad wouldn't notice if I got home at two A.M."

"Really?" Kevin stuck a sticky gob of cotton candy into his mouth. "Why not?"

"Kevin, we live in the hotel—year-round." Penny rested her chin on top of the baboon's fuzzy head. "My suite isn't exactly next door to my dad's.

It's not even in the same wing. So unless he happens to be outside when I get home, he'll never know what time it was."

Her suite? Whoa.

"So, you can do whatever you want?" Kevin asked.

"I guess," she said.

Kevin sneaked a peek at her. She didn't seem too thrilled about that. Every kid he knew would be beyond thrilled to come and go as he or she pleased. But Penny looked like that was about as great as eating liver.

"What's your dad like anyway?" he asked.

She didn't say anything for a second, and Kevin wondered if he'd touched on the *taboo* subject of the boss man.

Penny suddenly smiled. "He's great. He's a lot nicer than anyone would think. And caring too. He gives gobs of money to charities. I love my dad. I just don't see him too often."

"But you work for him," Kevin reminded her. "You must see him *all* the time."

"You ever see my dad when you're working?" she asked.

"No," Kevin said. As a matter of fact, Kevin didn't think he'd *ever* seen Mr. Booth except that one glimpse.

"So neither do I," she told him. "He's superbusy. Otherwise I'd probably see him more during the day."

"Well, at least you two have a lot to talk about at dinner if you don't see each other during the day."

"Dinner?" Penny let out a dry laugh. "I could

count on one hand the number of times I've had dinner with my dad since Memorial Day weekend. But that's okay. I mean, I understand. He's got a lot of business dinners and functions."

"So it's just you and your mom a lot of the time, huh?"

Penny stared at the ground. "My mom's in Europe for the summer. She's on a long vacation with her best friend. They're doing a different country every month. July is Italy. August is France. So, it's pretty much just me since I'm an only child." Penny coughed and ran her hand through her silky brown hair. "But enough about boring old me. I want to hear about you."

Kevin glanced at Penny. He was pretty shocked. Family was important to the Fords. He couldn't imagine his dad deciding to up and go on a fishing trip longer than *one afternoon,* let alone any kind of vacation, especially without his kids. He wanted to ask Penny how she felt about her mom and what living with her dad was like, but Penny had changed the subject in a way that told Kevin she didn't want to talk about it.

Her mom was a million miles away in another country, and her dad, though right here, might as well be a million miles away. Her family life sounded pretty cold to Kevin. And lonely.

So maybe being rich wasn't so great after all. Kevin's brothers might be annoying, but he'd die without Johnny and Danny nagging him and busting on him all the time. He loved them. And they loved him.

Penny's parents must love her too, he figured. *They just had weird priorities.*

Penny had turned quiet and thoughtful, so Kevin decided to stop it with the twenty questions and take the heat off her for a while. "What do you want to know?" he asked. "I'll tell you anything."

"Have you been spending the summer drawing during your free time?" she asked.

"I wish. I've mostly been practicing for the tourney," Kevin said.

"The tourney?"

Kevin explained about the volleyball contest and how much that prize money would mean to him and his brothers.

Penny nodded. "So winning the tournament is pretty important to you guys."

"Yeah," Kevin confirmed. "If we lose, Johnny's gonna have trouble paying his tuition for September."

Penny seemed lost in thought again. As her father's only child, she probably stood to inherit all that was his. Paying for college wasn't even a thought in her head. Was she thinking about how different the two of them were? How different the circumstances of their lives were? He couldn't tell. Having tons of money and all that money allowed you to do was probably something Penny didn't think much about. She didn't have to.

After they entered the hotel grounds, Penny stopped near the pool. She looked around, her gaze resting on the water. "Wow. I've never seen the pool so calm."

"Yeah," Kevin whispered. "It looks plastic."

The moon reflected off the surface like a soft white streetlight. Kevin didn't see anyone else on the patio. It was strange seeing it so empty. Usually there were hundreds of people running around and splashing.

Penny turned to him and smiled. Her features glowed in the light. "I'm glad I met you tonight, Kevin. And I mean that in every sense of the word."

He returned the smile. "Me too. I had a great time. I wish it didn't have to end."

"We have to work tomorrow," Penny replied. "It seems so far away."

"Let it stay far away," Kevin said.

Penny nodded. They didn't speak for a few moments. They looked at the moon, the pool, and each other. "Hey," Penny said. "Who says it has to end just yet? How about I whip up some virgin margaritas for us?"

"Virgin margaritas?" Kevin asked, liking the sound of whatever would prolong this evening.

"Yeah, you know, margaritas minus the alcohol," she explained.

Kevin smiled. "Sounds good to me."

Penny grabbed his hand and led him behind the bar. She set to work, and a few minutes later, she'd whipped up two drinks.

"Since you made them, I'll serve you," Kevin said with a wink.

Penny ran around to the front of the bar and sat on one of the stools. Kevin slid her drink to her.

"Here you go, Miss. The best virgin margaritas in Surf City."

Penny laughed and picked up her glass. Kevin picked up his own. "To us," she whispered, clinking her glass against his.

"To us," he repeated, staring into her eyes.

They each took a sip.

"Will I see you again?" Kevin asked.

"Tomorrow."

Kevin smiled. "Yeah, I know tomorrow. I meant—"

"I know what you meant, Kevin." She slowly moved in close to him. He could smell the delicate perfume she wore and the clean smell of the beach.

Kevin leaned closer—and knocked his drink over. It splashed onto Penny's shirt.

"I'm so sorry!" he said, quickly mopping up the mess on the bar with a bunch of napkins. He handed her some, but she shook her head.

"It's no big deal," she told him, smiling. "In fact, it was getting a little warm out here, anyway." She took off her shirt, revealing a flowered bikini top.

"Now, where were we?" she asked.

Before he could tell her she was the most amazing girl he'd ever met, she leaned over the bar and kissed him.

He wasn't expecting her lips on his. He clumsily slid his arms around her and returned the gesture as best he could from his position behind the bar. Kevin could feel the heat radiating from her body, the closeness of her form, her fingertips brushing the back of his neck. Her lips were so soft. He'd wanted to kiss her so badly, and it was now apparent to him that she had wanted the same thing. Kevin soared.

It was the perfect ending to the perfect night.

Until Kevin heard shoes grinding on the patio behind him.

And someone loudly clear his throat.

Penny broke the kiss and pulled away from Kevin. When she looked over her shoulder, her eyes widened, and she took in a sharp breath.

"Dad," she said.

Six

"**W**HAT DO YOU think you're doing?" came the booming voice of Austin Booth.

Uh-oh. The man was glaring at Kevin. Up close, Booth was taller than Kevin had thought. He stood a good six-two. Belly as flat as a plank. Even at midnight he wore a loose-fitting dark suit, a dark tie, and a shirt so white, it seemed to glow in the moonlight. The shadows made his eyes glint deep in their sockets. Booth's whole face was a mask of displeasure, deep lines, hard frown, and creased brow. Here, standing before Kevin, was a multimillionaire—the man who signed his paycheck. And here was Kevin, kissing his daughter.

What do I do? A jealous ex-boyfriend I could handle. I'd either get punched out or not. But how do I deal with an angry father/boss/millionaire?

Kevin tried to chill as he quickly exited from behind the bar and joined Penny, who stood, arms crossed, in front of the bar. First of all, Booth didn't know who he was. They had never met, and the chances of him knowing the faces of all his low-end employees were remote. So now it was just down to Kevin being a random guy who'd been standing behind the bar with a drink in one hand, a mess in front of him, while kissing his bikini-top-wearing daughter. If he was polite, maybe he could talk his way— Yeah, right.

"Dad," Penny began confidently, "this is Kevin Ford, a friend of mine. Kevin, this is Dad."

She nudged him forward. Kevin smiled and offered his hand. "Good evening, Mr. Booth—"

Booth ignored him and walked up to the bar. He took the drink and held it under his nose. "You're very lucky there is no alcohol in this," he snapped in an ice-cold voice at Kevin. "It's late, Penny. You're past your curfew. I want you inside, now."

Penny stepped forward, fists balled at her sides. "Dad, you didn't even say *hello* to Kevin. I always say hello to your friends when you introduce me to them."

Booth's eyes narrowed slightly. But that was his only physical reaction to his daughter's challenge. "So you do," he replied curtly. He leveled a stare at Kevin. "Kevin, how do you do."

"Fine, sir," Kevin replied. If he said he wasn't intimidated, he'd be lying through his teeth. "Just fine."

"Good." Booth nodded. "Now, if you'll excuse us, it's late. I'm sure your family is expecting you home."

Kevin shifted uncomfortably. By just looking at him, Booth had been able to tell Kevin wasn't a guest at the hotel. "Well, actually, sir, I'm staying down the boardwalk with my brothers. We have an apartment on the beach."

"Of course you do," Booth replied. "You better be off, then. The hotel grounds are closed to visitors after dark."

Kevin nodded. He made a move to leave, but Penny grabbed his arm.

"Dad," Penny said, "Kevin's hardly a *visitor*. He's my guest."

Booth took a deep breath, as if trying to contain himself. "Young lady, you are not to run around till all hours with strange boys you meet on the boardwalk. Nor are you to use this bar as though it were your own kitchen. I want you inside, *now*." He glanced at Kevin again and tilted his head toward the exit. "Good evening, Evan."

"His name is *Kevin*," Penny snapped.

Kevin winced and turned to Penny. "Good night, Penny. I had a good time."

Penny only nodded.

He felt a lead knot in the pit of his stomach as he went, but Kevin knew he had no choice. The longer he stayed, the worse it would be for Penny. So Kevin took a deep breath, plunged down the path to the boardwalk, and made his escape as quickly as he could without tripping over his own numb feet.

The Penny Booth Personal
Nightmare Quiz

Q: When deciding to make the first move with a guy, a girl should

(a) have an amazing time on the first date.

(b) feel really comfortable with the guy.

(c) make sure Dad catches you in the act.

(d) All of the above

Jen's gonna kill me when she finds out I circled *d*. Because Dad always comes outside to wait for me if I'm really late. It was as though I'd timed it perfectly.

Maybe I did. But not for the reasons Jen will think I did. Not because I wanted Dad to see me kissing Kevin Ford, cabana boy. Not because I wanted Dad to hit the roof.

But because I wanted my dad to meet the guy I'm so crazy about.

Does this make any sense? I'm not sure Jen will get it, and she's my best friend. But it makes sense to me. My dad is the most important person to me in the world besides my mom and Jen. And now another person could possibly join that group: Kevin.

I want the most important people in my life to know each other. Like each other.

Only problem is that—well, you saw what the problem is. Dad's gonna have more than a little trouble with the fact that his daughter's nuts about a towel fetcher.

The next day came very quickly. Kevin hardly slept at all. Before he knew it, he was in his white clothes, pushing a cart along the patio, placing towels on all the empty chairs and chaises. He smiled and nodded at the guests who acknowledged him, but he didn't dare speak. At one point he paused near the pool.

Unbelievable, he thought. *Last night I was standing right by here, kissing Penny Booth. Man, not bad. Not bad at all, Kev. Keep up the good work.*

He moved on, wondering what happened with Penny and her father. Was Austin Booth the type to ground his daughter? Not from what Penny had told him about her dad. But then again, the guy seemed to care very deeply about Penny, at least, as far as Kevin could tell from last night. Neither Kevin nor Penny had mentioned that she had met him at work at the hotel, so the man probably figured that Kevin had picked up his daughter on the beach like some random stranger.

Oh yeah, like that's worse than if his daughter's dating the loser who gets people towels and cleans their ashtrays, Kevin reminded himself. *Who are you kidding?*

You got work to do, so do it. Don't give the man an excuse to can you, he told himself as he wheeled his towel cart around the corner of a storage shed.

Just then Penny stepped in front of him and blocked his path.

"Hey, stranger," she said.

"Howdy, yourself," Kevin replied, smiling. "You still in your father's will?"

71

This made Penny laugh. "Don't worry about my dad."

"Thanks for not introducing me as one of his cabana boys," Kevin said. "He'd have freaked. I probably would have gotten fired."

Penny's eyes blazed with anger. "It's so unfair. But you've got nothing to worry about. He has no idea who you are."

Kevin nodded. "So, um, maybe I should keep a low profile. Make sure I don't call attention to myself if he happens to be walking around and shaking hands. Which means maybe we shouldn't be seen together out here."

Penny shrugged. "That's why we're behind the storage shed. Who's watching?"

"People hear things," Kevin said. "People see things."

"And those things might get back to my father, right?" Penny shook her head. "Don't sweat it, cabana boy."

Kevin absently stacked the few remaining towels on the cart. "That's easy for you to say, Penny. Your livelihood doesn't depend on your job."

Penny sighed. "Look, Kevin, my dad has his own ideas about which guys I should see. Ken dolls with sculpted hair showing Ivy League roots. Anyone else need not apply. But I have my own ideas too. He and I spar. No big deal."

"Maybe not to you," Kevin reiterated. "But I have to be careful."

Penny stepped around the cart and put a hand

on his cheek. The contact sent a chill through him. "Kevin, trust me. You're not even a blip on his radar screen. I like you. I want to see you again. Right now, if possible."

Kevin glanced around, feeling like a moron watching if anyone saw or heard what she just said. Why couldn't he just go with it?

"Hey, come on," Penny said, her expression full of concern. "Didn't you have a good time last night?"

"Of course I did," Kevin told her. "You know I did."

"Well," she said, a devilish smile playing on her lips. "We sort of got interrupted last night during a key moment."

Kevin grinned. "I think I know what key moment you're referring to."

Penny turned to the left, then to the right. No one could see them. She stepped close to him. He stepped even closer. And this time *he* kissed *her*.

Sweet. Creamy. Dreamy. He could kiss her for hours.

But the pool, which was surrounded by a gazillion people, was only a dozen feet away, around a corner. If someone happened to feel like walking near the storage shed, they'd easily see Austin Booth's daughter making out with some kid in a uniform. . . .

Still, all he wanted to do was kiss her. And kiss her. And kiss her.

Finally Penny broke the kiss and smiled at him.

Kevin grinned back. This was Penny, full force.

This was the girl he connected with last night. This was the only girl he'd ever lost sleep over. "So . . . you want to go out tonight? Do another chance meeting on the pier?"

Penny considered this for a moment. "How about I meet you at your place instead? I can meet your brothers."

Uh-oh. Inviting Penny into their low-rent world didn't sound very appealing to him. And his brothers could be obnoxious when they wanted to be. Still, Kevin was drawn to the idea for some reason. Maybe he really did want Penny to see where he lived. As low budget as it was, the apartment was Kevin's first real home of his *own*. He was proud of it in his own way. And it would be cool if his brothers met the girl he was falling for.

"Okay," he finally answered. "Sounds like a plan." He gave her the address, and they agreed on eight o'clock.

"Until then I'll see you around the pool, I guess," he said. "We can give each other signals. Like, a scratch on the elbow means: Meet me by the shed for one of those amazing kisses. . . ."

Penny burst into a laugh and disappeared behind the corner.

Dear Daddy,

I'm leaving you this note because I know I probably won't see you all day. I want you to know something: Kevin isn't just another boy to me. I really like him. I like him a lot. And I think you'll like him once you get to know him better. It wasn't his fault that I came in late last night. It was my fault. (Sorry.) Okay?

Love, Penny

"Hey, towel boy!" someone called.

Kevin sighed. Yep. He could kiss owners' daughters all he wanted. But after it was all over, that was all he was: towel boy.

Except to Penny. To Penny he was Kevin Ford, guy to like. Guy to date. Guy to keep dating? He hoped so. He couldn't get her off his mind. Like right now, when he was supposed to be running over to whoever had just called him, he was instead staring into space with a dreamy expression on his face. An expression that said: I just got seriously kissed by the prettiest, coolest girl in Surf City. . . .

A girl who was playing with fire by seeing him. But if they had to hide their romance to be together, then so be it. It was Penny he wanted. Not her dad's respect.

It suddenly struck him that Penny hadn't seemed intimidated by her dad. She hadn't begged forgiveness or rushed inside as Mr. Booth had commanded when he caught them kissing. She'd actually demanded his respect. And her dad hadn't screamed at her to do as he bid. He simply stated his case in a scary voice.

It was pretty cool the way Penny dealt with her dad. Without fear, but without being immature or crying or something. *She really is cool,* he thought.

"Hey, kid, move it already," the voice demanded. "I need something."

"Yeah, I'll be right—"

Kevin froze when he saw who had called him. *Oh, man, you have got to be kidding.*

Tanner St. John lounged in a chaise next to the pool, a syrupy tropical drink in one hand, a thick cigar in the other. His long, blond hair was spread out over his chest as if it was out to dry. His chest and legs were slick with oil. His swim trunks were flowery. And his grin was as wide and obnoxious as the Hollywood sign.

"Towel boy," he called again. "I need a towel, towel boy. My hands are greasy."

Kevin rolled his eyes.

Tanner chuckled. "Chop-chop."

Kevin groaned.

Tanner puffed on his cigar and sat up. "If getting me a towel is a problem for you, nose hair, I'll be happy to take it up with your boss. Being a new guest here, I'm sure my comfort is a little higher on the list than your job. See, I'm a VIP here now. You know what that means?"

"Vastly inadequate personality?" Kevin said.

Tanner eyed him. "Come on, Ford. Drop the resistance. You can't beat me at volleyball, you can't beat me at luxury, and you can't beat me at making you look foolish. So knock off the attitude and bring me my towel. Get it?"

Kevin wanted to spit on him. But he held it. In the end, as hateful as he found it, Kevin had to do his job and serve Tanner. So all he said was, "Got it."

"Then get it," Tanner ordered. "Right now."

Kevin retrieved a towel silently. He returned and handed it to Tanner, just like he would any other guest. Then he turned to leave.

"Oh, towel boy?"

Kevin grimaced. *Steady, dude. He's just working you. Don't let him dig in.* He turned and faced Tanner again. "Yes?"

Tanner wiggled his cigar at Kevin and smiled. "I seemed to have dropped my cigar ash. Sweep it up, please. It offends me."

Kevin peered underneath Tanner's chaise. Indeed, there sat a little plop of gray ash from his stogie. "I'll send someone right over to take care of it."

But before Kevin could turn away . . .

"Oh, towel boy?"

"Yes."

Tanner rolled the cigar around in his mouth and puffed huge clouds. "I'd like you to take care of it personally. And immediately."

Kevin moistened his lips and tried to keep cool. He had to. His job—his whole summer—depended on it. For some unfortunate reason, Tanner was staying at the Surf City. Which meant Kevin had to treat the jerk like a guest. Kevin's mind spun, thinking of anything, any way that he could get out of this. But nothing.

His eyes scanned the bar several yards away. Isaac, the head bartender, was just finishing with a brand-new tray of drinks.

Perfect.

"Excuse me, dude," Kevin muttered, and marched toward the bar.

"Hey!" Tanner cried, but Kevin ignored him.

Kevin went right to the bar and grinned. "Hey,

Isaac. Where do these drinks go?"

"Hey, Kev," Isaac replied. "You got them? Cool. Saves me a trip. They're for Mr. Gillespie's bridge game. Those guys just keep playing and playing and playing, man."

Kevin saw the game immediately: four old men dressed in twenty-year-old cabana wear, tossing cards back and forth at each other. Great. All he had to do was deliver the drinks, which would take him to the opposite corner of the pool, where he could avoid Tanner for the rest of the day.

He scooped up the tray, balanced it, and headed out. The ice in the glasses clinked and gurgled as he walked. Ugh. What were they drinking? The one cocktail was *green*. Kevin shook his head.

He walked by Tanner, brandishing the drink tray like a weapon and grinning. Tanner sneered back but didn't reply. He didn't have to.

Because his foot snaked out and clipped Kevin's ankle.

Kevin knew it was all over as soon as it happened. The foot. The tray. His balance. All over.

He hit the pavement hard. The cocktails spewed across the patio, tray clattering, glass crunching. He felt skin come off his knees and palms. Pain shot through his limbs, and he let out a loud groan.

Activity at the pool halted. All eyes turned to look at Kevin sprawled out on the pavement at Tanner's feet. There were whispers. A couple of chuckles. Kevin felt his face turning crimson with rage and embarrassment.

"Gee, I'm so sorry," came Tanner's lilting voice from above. "You're really not cut out for this job, are you? Maybe you should try flipping burgers."

Tanner burst out laughing and puffed heartily on his cigar. But even as Kevin got to his feet, he was already too late.

Penny marched right over to Tanner, yanked the tropical drink out of his hand, and dumped it on his head.

The crowd at the pool roared with laughter. Tanner's eyes bugged out as his hair, face, and cigar were saturated with fruit juice and chunks of mango. His jaw dropped open, and the now soaked cigar slipped free and bounced off his chest to the ground. His face screwed up in anticipation of his explosion, but when he saw that it was Penny, he paused.

"What's wrong, Mr. St. John?" Penny demanded. "Did someone dump a drink on your head?"

Tanner's whole body quaked. "You are so done."

Penny got in his face. "You want to repeat what you just said to me, motormouth?"

Tanner took a deep breath and wiped the drink from his eyes, slicking it back over his soaking mane of hair. "I think you heard me just fine."

"So that's what you say to an employee of this hotel after you abuse them?" Penny demanded, her voice carrying well across the patio. "After you deliberately trip them? I don't care what shade your American Express card is, Mr. St. John, but at this hotel, we do not tolerate that kind of behavior from our guests. You will treat our staff with respect, dignity, and common courtesy. Anything short of that will be considered a breach of your room agreement, and you'll be asked to leave." Penny dared a step closer to Tanner's dripping form. "Do you understand me, Mr. St. John?"

Penny was tough, but there was no way Mr. St. John would (*a*) let himself be humiliated the way he'd been and (*b*) let Penny talk to him that way. The jerk would probably run to Austin Booth's office and demand a free ride for this mistreatment by his pipsqueak, overzealous kid.

Kevin waited for the boom that was going to roar out of Tanner's ugly mouth.

But all the guy did was let out a deep breath. "I think we understand each other perfectly."

Huh? Kevin thought, staring from Tanner to Penny.

"Fine." Penny gestured at Kevin. "Now, apologize to Mr. Ford for tripping him. And I'm sure that you will reimburse Mr. Ford for any medical bills that may result from his fall."

Tanner's eyelids twitched, but his face remained cold stone. "You have to be kidding."

"Do I look like I'm kidding?" Penny challenged.

Tanner stared Kevin down for a minute. Then he glanced at Penny. Then, without saying another word, he yanked the towel from his chaise and marched toward the hotel. He wiped his head as he went, ignoring the smattering of laughter from the other guests. But other than those random sounds, everyone else kept quiet and returned to their business.

Kevin stooped and began tossing pieces of glass onto the drink tray. Penny joined him.

"Not bad, Miss Booth," Kevin said discreetly. "I should call you Miss Booth now, shouldn't I? You even have maniacs like St. John kowtowing to you."

Penny's eyes blazed with anger. "Yeah, you want to know why?"

"Uh, *yeah,*" Kevin said.

"Because that jerk wants to play in the volleyball tournament as bad as you do, Kevin. And who sponsors the tournament? This hotel. Which means, *my dad.* All I have to do is tell my father that a team member was abusing a staff member, and Dad'll disqualify the guy."

Kevin stared at Penny. Now, *that* was power.

"The jerk got what was coming to him," Penny added. "He checked in yesterday and has been nothing but an obnoxious jerk ever since. I overheard him talking to the front-desk manager. He'd been staying at a condo but wanted the luxurious hotel treatment. So now we're stuck with him."

"What about his buddies?" Kevin asked. "Arliss and Shooter?"

Penny shrugged. "I don't know them. Tanner's alone."

Kevin nodded. "Well, thanks for doing that. I wanted to. But something tells me I wouldn't be working here much longer if I had."

"Maybe everyone else at the pool will cut you a little slack now," Penny offered. "You never know."

A pair of white shoes appeared in front of Kevin.

He stared up into the face of Jake Hackman, his boss.

Kevin sighed and stood. "I'm sorry, Jake. The guy was out of control. He—"

Jake held up his hand. "That's not why I'm here, Kevin. I'm supposed to tell you something."

A twinge of apprehension flared in Kevin. "What's that?"

Jake's eyes betrayed his regret. "You're to report to Mr. Booth's office on the twenty-second floor. Immediately."

An Excerpt from Penny's Diary

This is really unlike me—sneaking away for a minute to write in my diary. But I'm really worried about Kevin. Why did Dad call him up to his office? It wasn't as though Kevin dumped that drink on Tanner St. John's head. And Tanner wouldn't make up lies to jeopardize Kevin's playing in the tournament, would he?

Maybe this has nothing to do with Tanner. Maybe Dad figured out that the guy he saw me kissing is a cabana boy at his hotel. Is he going to fire Kevin?

Oh God. Is that what's about to happen?

I'm standing in the very spot where I kissed Kevin earlier, by the storage shed. How I wish Kevin and I were standing here together, kissing again.

How I wish we could stand by the pool, hand in hand, and kiss to our heart's content in front of everyone.

Yeah, like I'll ever see that day.

I wish my dad understood me. If he did, he'd know that he was the one who'd raised me to judge someone by their character—not by how much money they have.

Funny. It's like he wants me to believe that but not live by it. And I can't be a hypocrite.

If Kevin gets fired, Dad's going to have to fire me too.

Seven

THE HOTEL FELT like a meat locker.

Kevin always spent most of his day outside. Inside, the air-conditioning was turned up so high that he wouldn't be surprised to see clouds of frost puffing from people's mouths.

Sometimes this place seems so surreal, he thought.

Like now. There he was, summoned to the top floor, the executive offices, to discover his fate. It hardly seemed fair. A few minutes ago Kevin was a hardworking member of a world-class service staff. But now, marching stiffly toward the elevators, he was just a fifteen-year-old kid with green liquor stains on his white shirt. A kid going to see the father of the girl he kissed behind the shed. It was like a bad movie.

He slipped into an elevator, punched the button for the top floor, and slumped against the wall. His eyes wandered to the tiny security camera in the ceiling. Was Austin Booth watching him now? Like some junior James Bond going to see Blofeld (put your feet against the sides in case the bottom drops out!)?

Kevin sighed. He just wanted to get it over with. He didn't even feel afraid anymore. Just a quiver of nervousness he associated with having recently sprawled across the pavement with a tray full of glass.

The doors opened on an opulent reception area. An attractive older woman with red hair sat behind the desk. Off to her left was a set of wooden double doors. To her right, a dark hallway. The woman nodded Kevin toward the double doors and told him to go right in. Mr. Booth was waiting.

Chop-chop, he thought grimly, remembering Tanner's obnoxious order. *Can't keep Mr. Booth waiting.*

The heavy oak door opened on a large, beautiful office. The whole room straddled the top of the hotel, offering breathtaking floor-to-ceiling views on both the east and west sides of the building.

So this is the office of a millionaire, he thought. *Very nice. Well, expensive, at least.*

The carpeting was a deep crimson. The paneling and furniture were made of the same wood as the doors. There was a small glass conference table off to the right. A credenza was to the left, a neatly stacked array of papers placed on its top.

The office was empty.

Guess Mr. Booth decided to keep me *waiting instead,* Kevin thought.

He wandered over to the ocean side of the office. Below spread the Pacific in its endless, white-capped march to the horizon. The beach was there as well—he could pick out Johnny's lifeguard stand (*if you could only see me now, bro*). Then there was the pool. From up here Kevin got a better idea of its strange, amoebalike shape. And it looked so much bluer from this height.

He even spotted the wet stain on the concrete where he'd spilled the drinks. The mess was gone, and so was Penny. But the stain remained. It seemed so far away that it might as well have been outlined in murder-scene chalk.

Just then a door opened from the far end of the office, and Austin Booth marched in. He held a sheaf of papers in his hand, which he scanned as he walked. By the time he got to his desk, he was finished. He dropped the papers in a pile and sat down.

He wordlessly gestured that Kevin should do the same.

No handshake was offered. Not a thing was said.

Kevin sat where he was told. The thick leather chair hissed as he sank into it. Kevin suddenly felt very self-conscious about the green liquor stain on his shirt. This was not a place for stains.

Finally, after scribbling on more papers for a moment, Booth set down his pen and leveled a stare at Kevin.

"Penny didn't tell me you worked at the hotel," he said sternly.

Kevin nodded. "I know."

"Which by its very definition is a deception," Booth continued. "A lie."

Kevin disagreed. But he certainly wasn't going to tell Mr. Booth that.

"My daughter and I have always been close, Kevin," he said, folding his hands in front of him. "Now, what relationship with a boy could possibly be so toxic that a daughter has to start lying to her father?"

Kevin shrugged. "I don't know, sir."

"That's a child's answer," Booth scoffed.

Kevin swallowed hard. *Okay. So that's how it's going to be.* It sure hadn't started promisingly. Why should Kevin expect things to improve?

He wants honesty, I can give him honesty. But he won't like it.

"My guess, sir, is that this has less to do with your rules regarding Penny dating her coworkers and more to do with *which* coworker she actually dates."

Booth nodded. "That's better. You should have said it the first time." He leaned back in his chair. "I didn't like what I saw last night, Kevin. Not one bit—"

"Oh, but that was—" Kevin began.

"*Is* never going to happen again," Booth cut in. "You're like any one of the hundreds of kids I've hired for the summer over the years. This is play time for you. You're having some fun, making some money, meeting girls, fooling around. You're looking for a good time, and you're looking for stories to bring back home with you. My daughter won't be one of those stories."

What a jerk! Kevin thought, his cheeks beginning to burn. "Look, sir—" Kevin began.

Booth cleared his throat, effectively silencing

Kevin. "I want you to stay away from Penny. Or there will be consequences. Such as losing your job."

The abruptness of the threat hit Kevin hard. Both the prospect of having to stay away from Penny and of losing his job.

Well, that's great, just great.

"Sir, we work together," Kevin said carefully. "It's going to be difficult—"

"If you want to keep your job," Mr. Booth grumbled, "then keep your head down and your nose clean. Do your job. Do not date my daughter."

Like any job was worth being told who he could and couldn't date? This man had to be kidding! Who did he think he was?

Okay, so he was a multimillionaire. So what! Big deal. There were other crummy jobs besides cabana boy at the Surf City Resort Hotel. He could flip burgers, cut grass, paint fences. Whatever. This wasn't the only job.

Well, okay again. Maybe it was. Danny had been fired a while ago and still hadn't been able to find another job.

Still, no one told Kevin Ford who he could date. And no one told Kevin Ford he wasn't good enough.

"Let me tell *you* something, *Mr.* Booth," Kevin began.

Booth stared at him for a moment. "I don't think I made myself as clear as possible. If you don't stay away from Penny, not only will you lose your job, but your brother—I believe his name is Johnny—will lose his job as a lifeguard."

A flash of alarm shot through Kevin. *Johnny?* "Mr. Booth, that's not—"

"*And* you and your brothers will be banned from competition in the Surf City 3-on-3 Beach Volleyball Tournament, which, as you know, is held on the grounds of my hotel."

Kevin didn't say a word. He couldn't. His whole world had just been put on the chopping block. And Booth was holding the ax.

The multimillionaire leaned forward on his desk, leveling a stare that was both menacing and amused. "You are not to date my daughter. Have I made myself clear?"

Kevin met his gaze, suddenly realizing that the game was up. "*All* too clear."

Booth nodded.

"Penny has no say in this whatsoever?" Kevin asked, frustration churning inside like acid.

Booth looked at his watch. "I don't believe that's any concern of yours."

Kevin held the man's gaze. "I haven't agreed to anything yet."

Booth cocked an eyebrow and slowly leaned back in his chair. "Don't fence with me. Your life in Surf City this summer can come to an end right here, right now. But you're smarter than that. I'm guessing you and your brothers need your jobs to pay your way, right?" He smirked. "And I'll bet Johnny needs that prize money for college. You want to throw everything away by standing up to me? No one will respect you for it, least of all me.

Choosing a girl over your family. No respect there, kid."

Kevin was about to point out how hypocritical Booth was being, but the second he opened his mouth, the man interrupted him.

"Keep away from Penny, and you get to continue your life as before. If you don't, I'll have you and your brother removed by security. Imagine *his* surprise when he's kicked off the job for, let's see. . . . How about talking to girls instead of watching the ocean?"

Kevin had never felt so angry, so powerless, in his life. "But—"

"But when Johnny finds out that you had the chance to save his job and his volleyball future and didn't . . ." Booth folded his arms. "Think about it, Kevin."

Kevin didn't have to think about it. There was no debate. He had to drop Penny, plain and simple.

"I'll assume your silence is an acceptance of my terms," Booth declared. He returned his attention to his papers and didn't look up again. He didn't say good-bye. He didn't say good riddance. He didn't say anything. Just kept scribbling.

Kevin quietly stood, feeling even more ridiculous in his green-stained whites, and slowly trudged to the double doors.

So this is power, he thought, staring one last time at Austin Booth's office. One man, one desk. All the decisions that affected hundreds of people came from here, right or wrong. In three minutes Booth had gutted and filleted the Ford brothers' lives on the desk before him. One answer and your scraps were fed to the dog. Another and you were allowed to live.

Kevin shook his head at Booth in disgust.

Power. Yeah. You can choke on it, pal.

Then he closed the door tightly behind him and left.

Eight

"**B**REAK UP WITH her tonight," Johnny ordered. "You said she's coming over here tonight, right? Perfect op, bro."

Kevin sighed and shook his head. Maybe he shouldn't have told Johnny and Danny what had happened with Mr. Booth. But when he'd turned up early (because Booth had given him the rest of the day off to think through his options), Danny had asked why he was home. The whole sordid story had poured out, and when Johnny had gotten home, Danny had gushed out the story.

After all, it was even more scandal filled than Danny's own reason for getting fired. The guy must have figured Kevin's predicament would take the heat off him!

Anyway, Kevin knew what they'd both say about the Penny situation.

Don't need a brain-surgery permit to figure that one

out, Kevin thought. He lounged miserably on the couch, tossing a volleyball up against the ceiling over and over.

Johnny had taken to pacing, like he always did when he got agitated (which only took him about three minutes once Kevin had elaborated on exactly what Austin Booth had threatened).

Danny sat in the lounge chair and stared at the Angels game on the TV. Kevin knew what he was thinking: *The world of work and women do not mix, so why bother working?*

"I can't believe this," Johnny muttered, pacing back and forth. "You two are jinxed when it comes to women. What, does dating make you feel the need to be unemployed?"

Kevin tapped the ball against the ceiling and caught it. "I haven't lost my job yet."

Johnny shook his head. "It's so poetic. I bust my hump all summer not only to pay the rent, but win that tournament, and inside of twenty-four hours my little brother goes on a date that destroys my life. One date. One good-night kiss. Hope it was a good kiss. A double lip smacker with tongue. Because it's the last one you'll be getting for a long time."

Kevin rolled his eyes. Johnny was one melodramatic dad type when he wanted to be.

Danny turned to Kevin. "No biggie, right, Kev? You're used to it."

Kevin threw the volleyball at Danny, who batted it away. "I went on a lot of dates last year, egghead."

"Knock it off, you guys," Johnny ordered,

kneading his fingers. "In case you haven't noticed, we have a bit of a crisis here."

"No, we don't," Danny replied wearily. "Because it's not even close to being a contest. Kevin dumps Penny. End of story."

"Wait a minute—," Kevin began.

"He's right, Kevin," Johnny agreed. "I can see the look in your eye now. You're trying to find some way around this thing. But there isn't one. You can't see this girl anymore. Not behind the shed, not behind our backs. It won't work. There's too many people who can find out, and there's too much at stake. Cut her loose. Now. Tonight."

A ball of anger swelled in Kevin's throat. "This is such a load of crap."

Johnny sat down on the arm of the sofa and spun the volleyball in his hands. "Dude," he said, his voice more earnest than angry now. "I know how you feel. But this is how rich people work. You see them every day. They play for keeps, even when it comes to something as stupid as towels. You know it's crap. I know it's crap. But we're in Booth's playground now, and he makes the rules. You're a threat to whatever master plan he has set aside for Penny. So step aside. He will crush you, bro. He'll crush all of us without a second thought."

"The guy doesn't even know me," Kevin said softly. "That maybe I'd be good for Penny. That we'd be good for each other."

Johnny smiled. "Such is the life of rich fathers and their only daughters."

"You know what?" Danny said.

Kevin and Johnny looked at his prone form in the lounger, a single corn chip caught in his shirt, the remote hanging limp from his fingers. "What?" Johnny asked.

Danny's eyes were lidded and tired. "The Angels are really lousy this year."

Kevin and Johnny looked at each other, blinking. "So what?" Johnny replied. "What does that have to do with anything?"

Danny shrugged; the corn chip fell off his belly onto the cushion. "All I'm saying is life could be worse. At the end of the summer we'll be able to say we accomplished something. Even if we don't win the tourney, we'll still have lived on our own, hung out with some cool chicks, and maybe made some friends too." Danny grinned. "Hey, Kevin. Even if you never see that girl again, dude, you had a great night with her. You found a girl who actually kissed you first. Do you know how rare it is for a guy of your limited personality and intelligence to get a girl to kiss you first? It's off the scale."

"Shut up, doofus," Kevin grunted, tossing a pillow at him.

Danny shrugged. "Remember it however you want to remember it. But I personally would tuck it away and make it a happy memory. Cut her loose like deadweight and remember the good times. That way we can all move on with the business of the summer." Danny sipped his soda and let out a belch. "Here endeth the lesson."

Johnny shook his head. "When do we get to hear the lesson about you finding a job?"

A lazy smile curled up Danny's face. "Some lessons take years to learn."

Their laughter was cut short by a knock at the door.

Kevin sat up, the lump in his belly growing hot. He glanced at his watch: five after eight.

Penny.

"Your door, dude," Johnny said fatefully, getting up from the arm of the couch and heading into the kitchen.

My door, dude. That's exactly right. Kevin got up, straightened his Coloursound T-shirt, wiped his nose, and crunched across the garbage-strewn floor.

"You go, stud," Danny muttered.

Kevin opened the door, and there she was. And he immediately regretted not canceling their date earlier that day. It would've saved him from the sight of Penny in a tight red cotton top and white shorts that accentuated the deep tan of her legs. Her hair was down, framing her beautiful face perfectly. Her smile nearly knocked him to the floor.

"Hey," she said, her blue eyes sparkling.

"Hey, back," Kevin replied, her smile spreading to his face. "Come in."

"If you dare," came Danny's warning from the lounge chair.

"Pardon the mess," Johnny explained, munching on a couple of Pop-Tarts. "Our maid took the

97

summer off." He smiled and extended his hand. "Johnny Ford."

Penny grinned and shook his hand. "Hi, I'm Penny. Nice to meet you. I actually feel like I know you already since I see you at the hotel."

"Small world, that hotel," Johnny agreed, nodding. "Everyone seems to know everyone over there."

That little arrow of a comment wasn't lost on Kevin. Man, it was hard enough to have to tell Penny they couldn't see each other anymore. He didn't need color commentary.

"That's Danny in the game room," Kevin said, pointing.

A hand rose and waved from the far side of the lounge chair, followed by a disembodied voice. "Hello, Penny. Excuse me if I don't get up, will you? I've been sitting in this chair all day and don't think my legs could handle the sudden weight."

Penny chuckled. "Quite all right."

"What my lazy brother means to say is he hasn't gotten up because he doesn't have to. He's unemployed, and his girlfriend was busy today."

"How nice," Penny replied, smiling uncertainly.

"How true," Johnny said as he walked by, returning to the couch with a fresh soda.

Kevin sighed nervously and gestured at the trashed room. "Well, this is casa Ford in all of its unshaven glory. What do you say we get out of here before we're overcome by fumes?"

Penny laughed and nodded. "Sounds good."

She waved at the inert forms in the "game room." "It was nice meeting you all."

"Bye/yeah/see ya/rock and roll," came the overlapping replies and waves.

Kevin rolled his eyes at Penny and quickly moved toward the door.

"You look great," Penny said with a smile as they exited the apartment building.

Kevin glanced at his clothes and wrinkled his nose at her. "A concert shirt and baggy shorts look great?"

Penny laughed. "Not your clothes. Just you."

Kevin gulped down the lump in his throat.

They opted for a walk on the beach. Kevin suggested it since the ache in his stomach only grew with each passing second at Penny's side. Especially since she took his hand not three steps onto the sand. Yeah . . . it had to be the beach. The beach was dark, so she couldn't see his face. It was quiet, so he didn't feel the need to fill every second with words. And in the end, it was private, since he knew in his heart that no matter what happened that night, he would be walking back to the apartment alone.

I've never felt so helpless, he thought. *So useless. I've got this wonderful girl at my side for the first time in my life—a girl I truly connect with—and I have to kill this living, breathing feeling inside me before it has a chance to grow. And why? Because a man with a lot of money says so.*

It wasn't fair.

Ah, but Kevin knew the follow-up to that phrase: *Sometimes life isn't fair.*

Well, that didn't cut it with him. Unfortunately, when you were fifteen, no one much cared what cut it with you and what didn't. Thus the unfairness of the world intensified.

"You're quiet tonight," Penny said, her voice a little more knowing than Kevin would have liked. Did she sense his churning gut?

"Just a really long day," he replied casually. "That dude Tanner has been around every corner. He really has it in for us."

"He thinks everyone is an opponent," Penny commented, her voice tinged with anger. "He's one of those idiots who always has something to prove."

"Do you know him?"

She shook her head. "No. But I know the type very well."

"I think . . . ," Kevin began, but faltered.

"What?" Penny's hand squeezed slightly, as if urging him to go on.

Kevin sighed. "I don't know. Maybe it's stupid. But I really think Tanner is afraid of us somehow." Then he chuckled. "I mean, not physically. He could wet his hair and kill me with it without trying. But there's something else. He knows there's something he can't touch in us. That must really chafe his shorts."

"He probably sees the good in you," Penny explained. "The intelligence and sincerity and wit that totally escape him. At least, that's the type."

Kevin kicked the sand. "I just hope we can beat him and his moron teammates. If not, he'll never let us live it down."

"There's more to life than a volleyball tournament, Kevin."

Kevin chuckled. "Not for me. Not this summer anyway. The prize money means too much. It's Johnny's immediate future. College and all. Plus volleyball is all the three of us have ever really had in common, aside from being brothers. That tourney's all I have motivating me this summer."

Penny stopped and turned to him. He could see her sly smile in the moonlight. "You have me."

The knife that had been working in Kevin's belly all night twisted hard. He knew what he had to do. And he knew he had to do it, without question.

Penny's arms slid around his waist and began pulling him close.

Kevin pushed them down and stepped away from her. He couldn't even look her in the eye.

Penny stood there, arms limp at her sides, staring at him. "What's wrong?" she asked.

"I can't do this," he replied, not sure if he was speaking to her or to himself.

You have to do this. Not for yourself. For your brothers. Their futures depend on you, bro. Just suck it up and do what you gotta do.

After all, who did Kevin want to get hurt: Johnny and Danny or Penny?

Neither and none. But that wasn't an option. He had to be loyal to his brothers. He had to give in to

101

Mr. Booth's arm-twisting demand. He had no choice.

"Can't do what?" Penny demanded, even though Kevin could tell she knew exactly what he meant.

"I can't see you, Penny," Kevin managed to say. His tongue felt as thick and dry as a log. "I . . . I just can't see you. Okay?"

"No, it's not okay," she replied. "I want to know why."

Kevin suddenly felt like such a chump. What was he supposed to say, exactly? *Because your daddy threatened me and my brothers, so you're history.* Was that it?

Penny's eyes narrowed. "Tell me why. Tell me the truth," she said, her voice cracking now. She stepped forward, pointing savagely. "My father told you you couldn't see me, is that it?"

Kevin stared at the ground. "Yes, and—"

"Duh, Kevin," she interrupted. "I know you were summoned up today to see the almighty this afternoon. He doesn't call people up there to have tea. He got to you. He doesn't want you to see me anymore, so he called you on the carpet, and you rolled over like a scared puppy."

Rolled over like a scared puppy? he thought angrily. *How dare she?* Did she think her father had said *boo* to him and he'd been scared out of a relationship with her? Was that how little Penny thought of him? He couldn't believe her!

"For your information—" Kevin started to say.

But Penny shook her head, interrupting him. "No, for *your* information, Kevin, I didn't think you'd bend over backward so easily for my father. But then, everyone does." She held her arms wide and let them flop uselessly to her sides. "Everyone does."

With that, Penny stormed away down the beach. Kevin's first instinct was to stop her, to chase her, to pull her back and hold her, tell her that her father had threatened his and his brother's jobs, plus the tourney. But he felt too sick to even call out her name. First her father had made mincemeat out of him, and now she had. He felt like both of them had taken something truly special and stomped all the wonderful stuff out of it until there was nothing. And now there *was* nothing.

He watched her silhouette grow smaller and smaller down the beach. In the distance the lights and echoes of the amusements teased him, reminded him of their first night together. Their only night.

Finally Penny disappeared.

You did it, Kevin thought. *You did exactly what you had to do. Now you and your brothers can do what you came here to do without interference. You're a little closer to understanding what it means to make adult decisions. Maybe it's good that you're both so angry at each other. That way, it'll be a little easier to be apart.*

But Kevin knew that was so wrong. It didn't feel easier. He didn't feel grown-up. He felt evil. He felt like he had betrayed the one thing he never thought he would ever betray: his heart.

So he just stood there for a while.

He just stood there and fought back the emotion that was rocketing through his system like a poison.

Fought it so hard that his whole body shook.

An Excerpt from Penny's Diary

I thought I knew what it was like to be rejected. After all, my mom's living it up in Europe for the fourteenth summer in a row. And my dad's deciding my life for me, without even wanting to know a thing about who I am. What I want. What I think. What I love.

And I think I just might love Kevin Ford.

Or maybe I could have loved Kevin Ford. But in the end Kevin kowtowed to the all-powerful Austin Booth. My dad probably threatened to fire him. Big deal. With my unfortunate connections, I could get Kevin a job somewhere else.

I don't get it. Kevin doesn't even like his job. So why would he choose to keep it and give me up?

Maybe Dad threatened him with something else. But what? Dad has nothing over him but the job.

I guess I deserve all this. It's true that I pursued Kevin in the first place to make Dad angry. I always hoped he'd be around the pool, shaking hands, whenever I talked to Kevin. But Dad was always somewhere else, as usual.

So just because Kevin's a cabana boy, he's supposedly not good enough for me. How does that make any sense? How does a guy working hard to earn a living mean he's not good enough? I just don't get it!

All I do know is that no matter what, I want Kevin Ford. For all the right reasons. And mostly because I'm crazy about him.

Nine

WHEN KEVIN HAD returned to the apartment, he didn't talk to his brothers. They did him the courtesy of not talking to him as well. Kevin knew they were giving him space, and he appreciated it. Both brothers had offered to give him their bedrooms for the night. But Kevin had told him he'd prefer to suffer on the couch to match his mood.

It had been a very, very long night.

The next day Kevin and Johnny arrived at work on schedule. Of the three words or so between them, exactly zero had to do with anything other than the bare necessities. Johnny immediately went about his business, leaving Kevin as he locked up his bike.

He was numb. Sleep had been like a fine mist to him, something that had dusted across his mind last night and hadn't registered as rest. He remembered no dreams. Only the nightmare he took to bed.

And the more he thought about what he did—and what it meant to his future—the more he felt like rearranging the furniture with a baseball bat.

Sure: Now that Penny was out of the picture, he and Johnny could continue to work at the hotel without interference. Sure: They could also play in the tournament, maybe even win it.

But Kevin had neglected to consider the fine print when accepting the terms from Mr. Booth (not that he was given time to read said fine print). First of all, he still had to haul towels for the snobs, take their abuse, pocket their cheap tips, and bust his hump for ten hours a day. And even worse? He still had to endure the sight of Penny as she took care of her own responsibilities around the hotel. Every time he'd see her, he'd flinch. Look away. Ignore her. Deny every impulse and feeling he ever had for her. He didn't even want to risk speaking to her, lest Mr. Booth be watching from above.

The bottom line? What kind of life was that? He didn't even like the cabana-boy job to begin with. Now it was made twice as miserable by seeing Penny, knowing full well he could never really "see" her.

As Kevin snapped his bike lock shut, he really, truly had to wonder if this employment opportunity of a lifetime was worth a second more of his time.

I'm a servant, he thought. *I'm dialed in for the duration. I can't quit. Johnny would go over the edge. Besides,*

I couldn't stay cooped up and unemployed next to Danny for the rest of the summer.

No. Quitting wasn't an option.

He made his way toward the front entrance to the hotel. Just then he spotted Tanner St. John. He was dressed in preppy tennis whites, his thick mane of hair pulled back in a ponytail (*I'd just once like to see him in pigtails,* Kevin thought). He walked with another man dressed in an expensive suit, a guy with a receding hairline and a mustache trimmed so close that it was hardly there. They talked in low tones, nodding and conferring like they were heads of state.

What's got Tanner so quiet and serious? Kevin wondered.

A black stretch limousine pulled up to the curb. The back door opened, and another man in a dark suit stepped out to greet the pair with warm handshakes. This guy was fat, with a thick helmet of brown hair and round, ruddy cheeks. He looked like he was used to greeting people and telling them what great things he'd heard about them.

Within seconds all three piled into the limo and slammed the door. The car pulled away from the curb and sped off.

So what's up with golden-boy St. John? Kevin wondered. *He didn't even stop to abuse me.*

"Guess everyone has their problems," Kevin muttered with a resigned sigh.

The day moved slowly. Towels changed hands. Dollar bills went into Kevin's pocket, the same people giving the same tips the same way every day. At least it was quiet. No Tanner sunning himself so obnoxiously that he could change his name to Tannest. No Mr. Booth hovering like a well-groomed Grim Reaper. And most important, no Penny.

Yet.

Kevin was both relieved and disappointed. He wanted to see her. Desperately. But he didn't want the flood of feelings that he knew would rush him as soon as he laid eyes on her. He didn't want to have to look away when she glanced at him. He didn't want to have to steal his own glances. But that's how it was going to be for the rest of the summer.

Deal with it, bro, Kevin told himself. *This is what you signed up for when you obeyed Mr. Booth.*

Where could she be? Sure, she might be avoiding him, but this was the first day since he met her that she didn't show her face in some official capacity. Almost like a cruise ship without the captain.

Soon after the lunch rush Kevin took his break at the bar with his usual, a bottle of spring water. He thought maybe he should eat something, but his stomach was still like a deflated balloon. Water was about all he could stand.

A few minutes later his boss, Jake, strolled up and sat next to him.

"Man, you must really have it going bad," Jake declared, smiling and shaking his head.

"What?" Kevin asked distantly.

Jake eyed him suspiciously. "Am I going to be firing you soon?"

"What are you talking about, Jake?"

Jake sighed. "Look, Kevin. You're one of my best workers and one of the few I can actually carry on an intelligent conversation with. So here's the deal. When Booth has to call you into his office, it's usually bye-bye, baby. Which means that I don't know why you're here today when he called you up yesterday. But if I'm given the word, you know I have to can you. And you also know that it won't be anything personal. I'd let you work here year-round if it was up to me. You're a good kid."

Kevin gaped at him. "Jake, what are you babbling about?"

"Booth wants to see you in his office, Kevin. Immediately. Again."

The fist balled around Kevin's insides squeezed for keeps this time. Rage boiled up inside him, the helpless anger that had no outlet. The rage Kevin had to just sit there and take. What did Booth want now? Did he think that his seeing Penny last night constituted some kind of official date? Even though Kevin used the time in a way even Booth himself could envy: ripping someone's guts out?

"You have to be kidding," Kevin muttered.

Jake shook his head. "Not this time, Kev. Just keep a stiff upper lip and remember that you're a good kid. Then let the bridges burn where they may."

"Thanks, Jake."

Kevin trudged into the cool refrigeration of the hotel lobby and punched the up button near the elevators. In seconds he was speeding toward the top of the hotel, once again the honored guest of Mr. Austin Booth, millionaire.

When the elevator doors opened and Kevin stepped into the reception area, he paused. The redheaded assistant was nowhere to be seen. Her desk was empty, the chair spun to the side (which seemed strangely chaotic to Kevin).

So what do I do now? he wondered.

He noticed the oak double doors were cracked slightly. He could see the glare from the big office windows beyond. Should he just go right in? Or should he wait and do it formally with the receptionist?

Screw it, he thought. *I'm not waiting around for this guy to torture me.*

Kevin gave the open door a nudge. It swung wide with a minuscule squeal, loud enough to announce his presence to the silent office. Nothing had changed in the twenty-four hours since his last visit. Except that this time Austin Booth was indeed waiting for him. Behind the desk Booth's massive leather chair had its back to him. It rocked slightly, as if Booth was sitting there pondering his next takeover with a child pirate's delight.

Kevin cleared his throat. *Show time.* "Mr. Booth? It's Kevin Ford. You sent for me?"

The chair stopped rocking. There was a pause. Silence. Then the chair spun around, and Kevin could see who was sitting in it, grinning at him.

Penny!

Ten

KEVIN DIDN'T SAY a word. He couldn't. He hardly believed what he saw: Penny, staring at him from across her father's desk like she was a powerful tycoon herself.

Maybe that's the idea, Kevin thought, gulping.

"Cat got your tongue?" Penny asked, reclining and putting her feet up. "Because I know you aren't shy."

Kevin cleared his throat. "Sorry. It's just that you weren't exactly who I was expecting. Did you put Jake up to it?"

Penny smiled. "No. I just let the grapevine do its work. Jake thought the message to report to this office was the real thing. I wouldn't risk getting Jake in trouble just because I wanted to see you."

Kevin nodded, understanding. "I get it. But it's okay if I get in trouble for seeing you, right?"

Penny's expression darkened. "Dad's out of

town until tonight, Kevin. No one knows you're up here but me."

"And Jake," Kevin corrected. "Either way, these things have a way of crawling down that grapevine you just mentioned."

Penny nodded, a scowl coming to her face. She dropped her feet to the floor and stood. "Kevin, whatever he threatened you with had to be really, really bad," Penny said. "Otherwise I know we would still be together."

Kevin nodded. "Bad doesn't even begin to describe it."

She stared at him. "I'll talk to him, Kevin. I mean, really talk to him. I need to at least make him try to understand my feelings. I don't know if he'll listen. But I've got to tell him that you're not just some summer fling."

Like *that* would make Booth happy! But it did make *Kevin* happy. Very happy. He did mean something to Penny. A lot, apparently.

Suddenly he was afraid to move. Afraid to say anything. Afraid to believe there was a chance for this thing to work. Maybe if Penny *did* have a heart-to-heart with her dad, their relationship would improve. Plus Kevin would get Penny.

"This never *was* just a summer fling," Kevin said. "I mean, I know you live here and I live, like, four hours away by car, but that doesn't mean I can't come see you."

Penny laughed.

That was funny? He stared at her for a minute,

then realized why she'd cracked up. "Oh. When I get my driver's license, that is."

They both laughed and looked at each other. There was nothing but warmth in Penny's eyes.

But then her expression turned serious. "What did he threaten you with?" she asked.

"Simple. Stop seeing you or I lose my job. And my brother Johnny loses his job. And my brothers and I are banned from competing in the volleyball tournament in August. Simple deal. Take it or leave it."

Penny's mouth had dropped open. She closed her eyes for a moment, then opened them. She shook her head slowly, emotion flowing through a tiny crack in her voice. "I don't believe him sometimes."

"Well, I believe him," Kevin replied indignantly. "And my brothers and I can't afford to lose our jobs and miss out on the tournament. We've spent months working toward this summer. It means too much."

Penny's blue eyes met his. "More than me?"

A wave of anger rolled through Kevin. "That's not fair, Penny. You don't know what it's like to have a future in doubt. But that's *all* I know. And bringing me up here to play your power game is putting everything at risk for me."

"No one will find out, Kevin," she said with a wave of her hand.

"People *always* find out, Penny. And when they do, it'll get back to your father, and the party's over for me. I can't believe that you'd jeopardize my life like this. Don't you care that I could lose everything just by standing here and talking to you?"

Penny toed the carpet, not answering right away. As if Kevin's words were truly sinking in. But then her gaze regained its intensity and again locked on his own. "I do care, Kevin. I care so much. But how can we let him do this to us? How can we let him win? We have to fight it, in whatever way we can. And if talking to him won't help, then we have to find another way."

She slowly closed the gap between them. Kevin wanted to step back, to turn and leave. But he couldn't. He was locked into her deep blue gaze and couldn't break away.

Because you know, he thought, *deep down, you know that you want to be here. You need to be here. Your heart raced when you saw her in that chair. It was relief and victory and exultation all wrapped into one moment. You wanted to see her. And now she wants to see you just as badly. She's right, dude. She's totally right. She cares about you, and she would do anything not to hurt you . . . except not see you. For that she'd risk anything.*

But he had to fight it. For his own sake. For his brothers' sake. His future . . .

"That's not fair, Penny," Kevin whispered, trying not to lose it. "You can't play master in my life."

"None of this is fair," she replied softly, so close now. Close enough to touch. Close enough to kiss. "We have to figure something out, Kevin. We can't just let him do this and that's the end of everything. No way. The rules have been stacked against us from the beginning. We've been breaking them, and we'll continue to if we have to."

"Penny—"

She interrupted him, her eyes blazing with emotion. "We have to find a way, Kevin. A way that doesn't let him touch you or your brother or the tourney. We're worth figuring out how to make this work. Right?"

His mind raced. He could smell the sweet waft of her shampoo, a delicate wisp of perfume. So nice. So perfect. It truly was the perfect moment. Late afternoon sunbeams slanted through the wide windows onto the red carpet, turning the office a deep crimson, creating another world. A world that made no sense. But it was their world. And for a brief moment, their rules.

Kevin wanted to believe that no one would find out about them. But he knew they would. He also wanted to believe that Penny didn't want him to get hurt. But he knew her recklessness put him and his brothers at terrible risk.

Both of those points brought him to one final question: *Was their relationship worth risking everything for?*

He couldn't just turn away from her. He'd waited his whole life for someone like her. And she wanted to be with him.

"This is so bad," he finally replied, stepping closer.

Penny smiled and reached out to him. "But so good."

They kissed, the deep red sun burning their

faces, submerging them in a world of heat and feeling that made Kevin pull her closer. She slid her arms around him and kissed him deeper. And all the danger and risk and emotion funneled into that moment, extending it, making it that much sweeter. Could it ever get any better with Penny? Kevin wondered. With anyone? He doubted it.

"I'm sorry," Kevin whispered, pulling back. "I wish I wasn't putting you in this position—to defy your own father."

Penny shook her head. "It's hardly your fault. It's not like we have a choice."

Kevin licked his lips, tasting her. His next words made the taste bitter. "I still don't have a choice, Pen."

Penny blinked. "What do you mean?"

Kevin pulled away and let his arms drop to his sides. "Nothing's changed, Penny. Even though we're seeing each other and it's great, your father wants me out of your life. If we're ever caught together, I'm done. My brothers too."

Penny groaned. "Don't remind me."

"I can't help it," Kevin replied with a shrug. "It's my *life,* you know?"

"I know." Penny returned to his arms and entwined herself around him. "So we'll just be extremely careful. I know Dad. He doesn't bother with things he can't see in front of him. And he's too busy to watch me all the time."

Kevin nodded, but his voice was grave. "You can be as careful as you want, Penny. But you'll still be Daddy's only daughter, no matter what you do. I have to be *more* careful. I have to be James Bond careful. No one's backing me up on this. So if I say we have to back off, we back off. Okay?"

Penny considered this for a moment. Then she nodded. "Okay."

"Promise?" Kevin pressed, and Penny smiled.

"I promise," she said.

They pulled each other close, and Kevin had never felt such a torturous combination of fear and happiness in his life. He knew what he was doing was very dangerous. But he also knew that he needed to do it, no matter what.

I can take care of myself, he thought.

But could Penny? Well, she said so.

As Kevin kissed her and held her closer than he'd ever held anyone before, he prayed she was right.

Instant-Messaging Transcript

Penny15: So Kevin and I made up today. We're going to make this work.

JenniferT: You two are really risking a lot just to be together. You must really, really like this guy, Pen.

Penny15: I think I'm falling in love.

JenniferT: Wow. This is so amazing. You and a cabana boy. Last summer you only flirted with staffers to make your dad go postal. Now you've totally flipped over one!

Penny15: I know. Kevin's so great! I can't wait for you to come home from camp and meet him!

JenniferT: Me too. Hey, so how can you be so sure no one will ever see you together? You could get ratted out anytime. Then Kevin and his brothers will lose everything, right? That's some risk. I hate to say this, but aren't you being a little selfish?

Penny15: I've agonized over that, Jen. But if Kevin's more important to me than my romance with him, how in the world am I supposed to just let him go without a fight?

JenniferT: I hate when you're logical. So is he a good kisser or what?

Eleven

AFTER WORK THE boardwalk was too busy for bikes. The sun sank toward the Pacific, lighting the horizon on fire and laying a bed of coals that reminded all that their suppers were cooking. The mealtime rush of tourists clogged the restaurants and pizza stands up and down the thoroughfare, everyone chomping and slurping and meandering like the vacationers they were.

Kevin and Johnny rode the streets home. The car traffic was heavy and slow, but they rode the bike lane at a steady pace. It had been a long day for both of them, and it showed in their pedaling. But Kevin hardly felt the road beneath him. He was still thinking about the office and Penny.

I'm so stupid, he thought. *I can't believe I let her pull me into this web. If I mess up, it's all over. But still . . . if we can somehow pull it off? It'll be sooo worth it.*

"Why so quiet?" Johnny asked, a faint sheen of sweat on his brow.

"Nothing to say," Kevin replied.

"How'd you do today? Tips, I mean."

Kevin chuckled. "Why? Am I buying dinner again?"

"No," Johnny replied tediously. "I'm just curious."

"Since when did my financial life become any business of yours?" Kevin grumbled.

"The same time your love life did," Johnny declared. "Because last night you told us in no uncertain terms that your love life was suddenly hog-tied to your financial life. I just want to make sure you're cool with everything."

"Everything?" Kevin asked.

"You disappeared for about an hour this afternoon," Johnny pointed out. "Jake Hackman mentioned that Mr. Booth called you to his office."

A wave of panic shot through Kevin. *They know already. Play it cool.* "So?"

"So . . . what did the man say? Does he know you broke up with Penny last night?"

Kevin's mind raced. What should he tell Johnny? The truth would only make him angrier. But maybe he knew the truth already. Maybe he was just torturing Kevin now. . . .

"I don't know what he knows, Johnny," Kevin replied. "I don't want to think about Mr. Booth right now."

"I heard he was in LA today on business," Johnny continued, pedaling easily. "Something about his restaurant in Beverly Hills."

"Yeah, some celeb broke some plates or something," Kevin said casually.

"Mmm–hmm," Johnny agreed. "I heard that too. Which is strange."

Kevin's belly churned. "Why's it strange? Celebrities are always smashing stuff and trashing rooms."

"Not about the celeb," his brother corrected. "It's strange that you'd get called up to Booth's office when he's not even *in* his office. And that you would disappear for almost an hour."

Kevin glanced at Johnny. His brother stared at him, only checking the street in front of him enough to keep from crashing.

"What's your point, bro?" Kevin demanded, but he already knew the answer.

"You're still seeing her," Johnny said, his voice full of accusation.

Kevin sighed, watching the street pass beneath his tires. "So what if I am," he finally replied.

"So what?" Johnny exclaimed. "So what? Are you kidding? You know exactly so what! She's bad news, Kevin. She's the worst news. She'll get us canned."

Kevin shook his head. "Not if her dad doesn't find out."

"How's he *not* going to find out? You couldn't even pull off seeing her today without me figuring it out. How much harder do you think it will be for Booth to find out? Someone always sees, bro. Someone always talks."

"I'm being careful," Kevin said, hating how lame he sounded.

"You're an idiot," Johnny replied flatly. "You have absolutely no idea what you're getting yourself into."

Anger finally took over. Kevin couldn't hold back anymore. "I do so! I know what could happen if we get caught. We'll lose everything. Our jobs, the tournament, everything. But I also know that this is totally bogus, and Penny agrees. Her father has no right to keep us apart just because I'm from some blue-collar nightmare of his. We're not going to let him do that. We're going to be really, really careful, John. I swear it. Penny means a lot to me, man."

Johnny only shook his head. "You don't get it, bro. You really don't. Don't you hear the talk around the pool and at the beach? Everyone knows Penny at the hotel. And everyone knows what she's really like. And why she really likes you."

Frustration boiled in Kevin. "What are you talking about, Johnny?"

"It's not just that her dad can have us dumped from the tourney," Johnny said. "It's Penny. She's only chasing after you to tick off her dad."

Kevin rolled his eyes.

"Penny dates working-class guys like you to make her father angry," Johnny explained. "She picks a guy working at the hotel and flirts with him. He asks her out. They go on one date, and she makes sure Daddy sees. Then Daddy flips and finally pays attention to the poor, little rich girl."

Kevin scowled and shook his head. That didn't sound like Penny at all. "No way, man. That doesn't make any sense."

"It's true, Kev." Johnny adjusted a rattling gear on his bike. "She did the same thing with Joe Talbot last summer. You know Joe?"

Kevin nodded. Talbot had been a waiter at the hotel restaurant who had worked several summers in a row. That summer, though, he'd quit at the end of June. No one knew why.

"Last summer Daddy's little girl came home from camp to slum," Johnny said. "She burned Joe, and he couldn't deal with seeing her again. So he quit. She's done the same thing every summer since she was thirteen, Kev. She picks a waiter or a cabana boy—anyone who seems blue-collar—and runs him through her father's paper shredder."

"I don't believe it," Kevin said. "Where did you hear all this?"

Johnny rolled his eyes. "I heard two girls talking about it on the beach today. Man, I was so happy to know that you'd dumped that chick. So you can imagine I'm not too happy to hear she's still playing you. Playing you *so* bad that you're willing to risk the tourney for me and Danny. Stay away from her."

Kevin shook his head. "So basically I'm the new lowly loser, is that it? Well, that's crap, Johnny. Total crap. She really likes me, and I like her. It's that simple. She's risking a lot by seeing me and vice versa. But I think she's worth the risk."

Johnny groaned. "Haven't you heard a word I just said?"

"I'm not just another working-class zero to her, Johnny. I'm telling you."

"Okay, fine," Johnny said, exasperated. He paused to swerve around a pedestrian. "If she likes you so much, why doesn't she care what *you* might lose by seeing her?"

"She does," Kevin said defiantly. "We think it's worth it."

"That's easy for her to say," Johnny muttered. "She doesn't have anything riding on this summer. On our jobs. Or—"

"On the tournament, yeah, I know," Kevin finished. "Bottom line, Johnny, I think you don't want me to see her because of that stupid tournament."

"That's right, Kev," Johnny agreed. "I don't. Don't go down this road. Danny went down it with Raven, and we almost killed each other. You know what the tournament means. Don't blow it like Danny almost did."

"Danny didn't blow it," Kevin reminded him bitterly. He gripped his handlebars tight, feeling the sweat that had accumulated there.

"This is different, man," Johnny pressed. "No one was holding an employment ax over Danny's head. He wasn't going to lose anything if he continued to see Raven. You will."

Kevin shrugged. "I'll quit my job. Then her old man can't say anything about Penny dating a cabana boy."

Johnny's voice was nearing the breaking point. "He'll still bar us from the tournament, Kevin! Don't you get it? There's no way around this. You *have* to cut her loose. If you don't, we're all done. And I didn't come all this way to lose everything over a rich girl trying to rebel against Daddy."

"Just let me handle it, Johnny," Kevin replied. He tried to sound forceful, but it came out hollow, and Johnny picked up on it right away.

"Right, whatever," he said with a bitter laugh. "You go and handle it, little bro. Impress us all."

Kevin didn't answer him. They didn't speak the rest of the way to the apartment. Kevin rode robotically, automatically weaving through pedestrians and cars. All he could think about was what Johnny had told him.

Did Penny only date him because he was a "loser"?

Did she only want to rebel against her father?

Was she lying about *everything*?

No. Not a chance. Not after this afternoon. Penny couldn't be seeing him just because he didn't have a lot of money . . . just because she knew Daddy wouldn't approve. Not after the scene in her father's office. Those kisses couldn't lie.

Could they?

Twelve

THOUGHTS TWISTED THROUGH Kevin's mind all night like worms. By the time he had himself convinced of one thing, all the doubts paraded in front of him again, forcing him to change his mind.

He simply didn't know who to believe. On the one hand, Johnny had every reason to want Kevin to dump Penny: the Fords' futures depended on it. But on the other hand, Kevin couldn't believe that Penny was using him. She was so sincere, so genuine, so passionate when she was with him. He couldn't just be a loser for her collection. A plaything to be flashed in front of her disapproving father. It just didn't add up.

He'd done nothing but think about it all night long. "S'okay," he mumbled as he stumbled out of bed the next morning. "Sleep's overrated."

Kevin spent the day dealing towels to the masses and

rubbing the gray, meaty bags under his eyes. He didn't see Penny or Mr. Booth all morning. In fact, it was as quiet a day as he could remember. No one looked at him strangely. No one tittered when he walked by. No one was gossiping about him and Penny.

Johnny's so full of it, he thought as he lugged two garbage bags toward the Dumpster on the side of the hotel. *I don't know why I listen to him at all.*

But before Kevin could turn the corner to the Dumpster area, he heard a loud bang and some laughter ahead. Then he heard the unmistakable voice of fellow cabana boy Charlie Smith. "You know why," Charlie was saying to someone. "Penny is a total hottie, a total flirt, and a total slot machine just waiting to pay off. I'd do the same thing if I was the Kevster."

Kevin froze, his eyes narrowing. The *Kevster?*

"I still think Ford's being an idiot," came a second voice that Kevin recognized as that of Frank Smith, a janitor. Anger seethed in Kevin. But he held his tongue, stepped back into a shadow, and listened. "I mean, he thinks she's really into him? Give me a break. A chick like that goes slumming among us for kicks. Just like she did last summer with Talbot. And the summer before that with the pool cleaner's assistant."

"I wonder if big-man Booth knows she's seeing Ford yet," Charlie said. "The man'll go postal! That's probably what Penny wants, though. The whole thing makes me sick."

The Kevster backed away from the scene, leaving

the two garbage bags where he was standing. His mind was a slow-rolling boil.

It's true, he thought, his insides going numb. *It's all true.*

Kevin abandoned the hotel. He had to think. He couldn't do that while he was worrying about towels or running into Penny or, worse, Mr. Booth. He knew going AWOL was a dumb thing to do, but he really didn't think Jake Hackman would fire him. Even if he did, it wasn't like Kevin was on the top of the cabana-boy promotion list anyhow. At this point Kevin really didn't care if he got canned. The hotel could fall into the sea, and he'd feel relieved.

Kevin slipped out onto the boardwalk and onto the public beach. Eventually he found himself leaning against a piling underneath the amusement pier. The surf pounded against the other pilings, splashing and whooshing like a loudspeaker at a shuttle launch.

All Kevin could do was fight off the lump in his throat, stare at the waves, and massage his rage.

Penny is using me, and everyone knows it. Everyone. Those Dumpster doofuses. All the guests probably know too. My brother sure does. Johnny tried to tell me, but I didn't want to listen. But now I know. . . . It's true.

Kevin didn't know what to do. Thinking was all he came up with, but even thinking took all his concentration. There was so much anger, so much emotion, all he heard was a whooshing in his ears; his blood, not the surf.

All of it made sense, actually—if he thought

about it rationally, that is. The first kiss that night by the pool. The kiss behind the shed. Penny constantly looking around to see if someone was watching. The setup in Mr. Booth's office. Those were all orchestrated by Penny. All of them took place in locations that could be easily monitored. The kisses could be seen. They could then be spread to the public. Or even better, Mr. Booth could catch them red-handed, like he did that first night.

Everything designed so Penny's father would hear about it.

What would make her do this to me? Kevin wondered desperately. *Where did all her anger come from?*

It was probably a combination of things. The money was a big one. Kevin spent enough time around the rich guests to know what money did to your perceptions. Some people counted more than others. And Kevin's paycheck was like a ticket on that blue-collar express straight into the jaws of the wealthy.

In the end it didn't matter why she did it, just that she did.

But those kisses, that passion and sincerity . . . was it all an act?

Kevin drew in a deep breath and balled his fists, wishing he could punch a pier piling without shattering his bones.

Act or no act. He had to find Penny and settle this thing once and for all.

He found her in the lobby. Penny was smiling and pointing out one of the hotel's restaurants to a

132

foreign couple. She smiled wider when she saw Kevin. The couple thanked her and moved on. Penny didn't pick up on Kevin's determined expression. Not at first.

"Hey, you," she said, hugging a clipboard and trying not to be too obvious. There were other guests and employees around, after all. "How's it going?"

"We need to talk," Kevin said curtly. He didn't return the sunshine and smiles.

Penny eyed him for a moment. Then she jerked her head toward a hallway off the main lobby. "Come on."

They walked down a spartan hallway meant for employees only. The luxurious furnishings and marble floors transformed into gray fireproof carpeting and white walls. Penny led him past several offices, through another door, then down a shorter hallway to a steel door. She pushed it open, and they went inside.

They were in a fire stairwell. The earthquake-proof concrete floor was painted battleship gray. The steel beams of the stairs were a glossy black. Single fluorescent bulbs burned every few feet, throwing a harsh, hard light that hid nothing on a person's face.

"What is it?" Penny asked, her voice full of concern. "Are you okay?"

Kevin shook his head. "No. Pretty far from okay, Penny."

She took a step forward, touching his arm—a prelude to taking his hand. Which would be a prelude to who knew what. *Steady,* Kevin told himself. *Do not let her take control of this situation. You aren't in the right frame of mind to resist her if she makes contact.*

He stepped back. Penny was noticeably surprised by this.

"Kevin, what's—"

He held up a hand. "I know what's going on, Penny."

"Know what?" Penny shook her head in confusion.

"I know . . . I know why you've been seeing me." Once Kevin actually said it, the rest flowed easier. His anger took over. "I know that every summer you pick up some guy from the hotel who doesn't have a lot of money. You do it just to get under your dad's skin. That's why you came on so strong to me. That's why it was so *easy* for you."

Penny gaped at him. "Kevin, it's not true—"

Kevin stared at her. "I'm dead serious. Don't play dumb. It's an insult to my intelligence. I've heard all about it from more than one source." Kevin leveled an even nastier stare. "You used me, Penny."

Penny blinked, swallowing. She didn't answer at first.

Is she thinking up a dodge? Kevin wondered. *Or is she just surprised that I found out the truth?*

When she did answer, her voice was low and soft. "I . . . I never meant for you to find out about the other guys. I couldn't have told you about that, Kevin. About how I used to be. Before I met you. Before I—" Penny paused, and Kevin saw her eyes were shining with tears. "Maybe in the past I dated a few guys to get my father's attention. But—"

Kevin's eyes narrowed. "You have to be kidding. I find out that you churn and burn a different working-class guy every summer for the past three years, and I'm supposed to believe that it's somehow different with me?"

Penny nodded vigorously. "It's true, Kevin. It really is. Don't you believe me?" She took a step forward, forcing him back again. "Don't you?"

The anger seeped up into his belly again. "Do you know what I risk by seeing you? Do you know what your father will do to me and my brothers if he catches us together?"

Penny's shell hardened slightly. "I'm well aware. You remind me of it every minute."

"People's jobs are on the line, Penny. Even if we don't see each other, how do you think I can work around here anymore? It'll be impossible. We're right on top of each other all day. How am I supposed to act like you're not my girlfriend?"

"Am I your girlfriend?"

Kevin stared at her. The anger seeped out of him. He was tired. Tired of everything. "The whole thing's been a setup from the beginning. You and me. Your dad finding out. But your little fun and games went too far this time, Penny. You weren't just the cause of some poor schlepp quitting a good job. You put my brother's future on the line. All for kicks."

"It's not like that, Kevin."

"Oh, come on." Kevin gestured at the concrete

walls around them. "What about this stairwell? You dragged me down here in two seconds. Is this one of your little hideaways? Or will your dad come tromping down from the penthouse any second now?"

"Now you're being silly," Penny whispered. "And mean."

Kevin straightened and folded his arms across his chest. "Look me in the eye and tell me that none of it is true. If you can do that, I'll back off."

She paused, not meeting his gaze. Then she slowly nodded. "Maybe it was true the first day I met you. But you totally hooked me, Kevin. I've never met anyone like you. You're real. You're not like the fake trust-fund twerps my father is always trying to fix me up with. And you're not even like the other working-class guys I dated. You're you. You're funny, and cool, and smart, and talented, and you think about things. You understand people." She met his gaze head-on. "I really do care about you, whether you believe it or not."

Kevin sighed angrily. "How can I trust you? Everything has been planned from the very beginning. I feel like I'm just a piece on a Monopoly board. Your father owns a hotel on Boardwalk, Penny. Think about it."

"Kevin, I'm telling you. It's not like that."

"Oh yes, it is," he snapped. "You date me to tick off your father. Your father lowers the boom on me, I lose my job, my brother loses his, and we're out of the volleyball tournament—our one ticket in this stupid lottery. Well, I've had enough. I don't want to lose my job. I don't want to let my brothers down. They're my family. And family always comes first." Kevin looked her straight in the eye. "Just like with your father."

Emotion clogged Penny's voice. "That's not fair."

"Fair, accurate, and damn straight. You use people, Penny. You used me. And I could've lost everything because of it. You say that's not what happened, but it was. You say you didn't mean it, but guess what? I don't believe you." Kevin let out a deep sigh. "I just don't believe you, Penny."

Before she could reply, Kevin turned, yanked open the steel fire door, and walked out.

He was grateful that she didn't follow. He didn't know what he would've done if she had. There was nothing left inside him. His guts were torn out. His heart was shattered. He hated the summer. Hated the hotel and Penny's father. He hated what she'd tried to do to him, and he hated her for her deception.

But most of all, he hated himself for what he just did to her.

An Excerpt from Penny's Diary

I guess Kevin's right. I did go too far. I should have known that someday the stupid, immature way I used to go about getting Dad's attention would blow up in my face.

But all I ever wanted was my father to love me. Care about me. Want to spend time with me. And all he ever wanted was to spend time with clients and business associates. I just don't figure into his life in any real kind of way. Except when it comes to who I date. Then suddenly he's Mr. Concerned. He spends an hour lecturing me. How would I ever get an hour of my dad's time otherwise?

So now my whole relationship with Kevin blew up in my face. I can't believe how he tore into me today. And I can't believe how much I deserved it. I always knew that he was different from all the other guys I've dated, rich or poor. He's sweet. Fun. But most of all, real. Today he proved it. He showed why he is such a better person than me. And why I don't deserve him.

I could blame Dad. All this started because he

wouldn't let me see who I wanted to see. But blaming him would be too easy. I'm the one who lied. I'm the one who used people. I'm the one who set up situations so Dad would find out about them.

I should've faced him a long time ago. But I was too much of a coward. Now it's cost me Kevin, a guy I'm in love with.

Yeah, that's right. In love with.

All I can do now is ask myself, "How do I fix everything?"

Thirteen

KEVIN COULDN'T BELIEVE he was still working. But in the end, when the accusations stopped flying and things got quiet, there were always more towels.

That should be written on a bathroom stall somewhere, Kevin thought morbidly. *Words of wisdom.*

This day had turned into one of the worst he'd ever had. And it was barely three o'clock! The six-to ten-year-old heirs of American industry still splashed and screamed in the pool. Their aloof mothers and nannies lounged demurely with their nails painted and their lips pursed. And they all needed what Kevin had to offer. They all needed a humble smile and a drink. They all needed shrimp cocktails. They all needed to hear the words "right away, ma'am/sir." They all needed—*absolutely gosh-darn required*—fresh towels.

Here I am, folks, Kevin thought with a defeated

sigh as he surveyed the patio crowd. *Use me.*

When the towel supply ran low—like it just had—Kevin or some other cabana boy usually marched right down to the hotel laundry and brought back a new supply stacked neatly on a rolling cart. Last time Kevin checked, the cupboards in the towel shed were looking bare, so he fetched a cartload, wheeled it back to the shed, and started stacking bleached white towels on the shelves, one after the other. One day Kevin vowed he'd count them to see just how many towels he went through in a day. But not today.

The inside of the shed was about the same size as their kitchen in the apartment. There was an overhead light, many shelves on either side, and a well-stocked supply of amenities designed to anticipate whatever a guest might request: suntan lotion, umbrellas, sunglasses, electric fans, water bottles for spritzing away the heat, and an array of water toys for both kids and adults. But the main function of the shed was towels. Towels made the world go round. Towels made people happy. Towels made the perfect free souvenir.

Maybe I should grab a few of these puppies myself, Kevin mused, stacking and stacking. *Better than the scrap of cloth I have back at the tenement. Maybe I could get Johnny and Danny to pay—*

Loud laughter broke his train of thought. Kevin poked his head out of the shed to see what the problem was. But there was no problem—no problem, that is, as long as Kevin stayed in the shed.

Tanner St. John and two other men had taken up a roost at an umbrella table just outside. They were all dressed in tennis whites, laughing and sharing drinks. One of the men smoked a fat stogie.

Then Kevin recognized them—one was the guy Tanner got in the limo with the other day. The one with the supertrim mustache and male pattern baldness. The third one was the man already in the limo—the heavyset man with the thick helmet of hair and red cheeks. They chatted and chuckled some more, but Kevin thought the laughter was more good-natured than real. Salesmen's laughter.

"So the deal is all but signed, Tanner," Mr. Mustache declared, sipping his drink. "It's going to be a great thing for you and this hotel."

Mr. Helmet nodded, puffing his cigar. "You have a very bright future, young man. Fizz Cola is happy to be a part of it."

More chuckles, drinking.

Fizz Cola? Kevin wondered. *What's Tanner got to do with Fizz Cola?*

"This deal sounds real sweet, David," Tanner said, speaking to Mr. Mustache. "The money's sweet. The suite is sweet"—more chuckles—"but I have to ask why Mr. Booth isn't in on this. I mean, it's his hotel, right?"

David scratched his cheek absently and didn't miss a beat. "As director of marketing for the hotel, Tanner, it's my responsibility to line up deals similar to your own. Mr. Booth isn't involved at this level." David snickered. "He's more interested in buying up beachfront property and overdeveloping the city."

Mr. Helmet shook his head, puffing smoke. "In all candor, gentlemen, I've dealt with Austin for several years now. It took me two years to sell him on Fizz Cola. He just doesn't see what's hot and what's not. Which is why he would never see an exclusive partnership sponsor deal like you're signing, Tanner, as worthwhile."

"Mr. Booth is not, as they say, on the cutting edge," David added coldly. "In fact, sometimes it seems he's more interested in things like what his daughter is doing than how much money he's making."

The trio laughed at this. Kevin's face grew hot. Did *everyone* gossip about Penny?

But still, this was interesting. What "deal" were they talking about? Why would a hotel exec, a Fizz Cola rep, and Tanner be talking about "sponsor partnerships"?

"The boss needs to watch more MTV," David commented. "Summer happens all year-round in southern California. The pro-volleyball tour deserves this hotel and its resources for its competitions. The tournament this August will prove it."

"And you, Tanner," Mr. Helmet said, "will be its next star."

"As long as you and your boys win the tournament," David warned. "You don't win the tourney, you don't get the deal."

Tanner flashed his surfer-boy grin and ran a hand through his Fabio hair. "It shouldn't be a problem, David. I've already played against the competition. It's gonna be a turkey shoot." Tanner sucked his straw until the drink gurgled. Then he smiled at Fizz Helmet. "Just be sure to bring your checkbook, Mr. Greech."

Fizz Greech smirked and raised his glass. "As long as you bring a trophy, Tanner."

"It'll be a pleasure," Tanner said. "I've done all I can do at the college level. Now it's time to think big and go pro. It's just a shame that this tournament's booty won't count toward my tour winnings for the year. Winning the most money gets you a nice trophy too."

"Don't knock it, Tanner," David said. "It took a lot of doing for me to get an exemption from the college athletic office. Normally they don't allow amateur players to compete for money."

"Let alone ten thousand dollars from Fizz Cola," Greech added grandly.

"But the athletic office understands the need to attract the best amateur talent in southern California," David went on. He held up a cautionary finger. "That's why it's crucial that your deal with us remain a secret. By signing this before the tournament, you're giving up your amateur status, which would make you ineligible." Then David's salesman smile appeared again. "But you're a smart guy. And a great player. You know what to do."

Tanner smirked and nodded. "Just win, baby."

The three men roared with laughter and clinked their drinks. Kevin used the distraction to slip out of the shed and away from the group.

The laughter echoed across the patio as Tanner dramatically scribbled his name at the bottom of a thick sheaf of blue paper and Kevin made his get-away.

"That's just perfect," Johnny grumbled, staring out at the empty surf. He was still on duty, leaning against his lifeguard stand, even though at four in the afternoon no one was in the water. "So Tanner makes a run for our cash and goes pro with a Fizz sponsorship to boot. That's just great." Johnny sighed. "How much is the endorsement contract for?"

Kevin shrugged. "They didn't say. You think Tanner's worth six figures?"

"Only if he washes his hair before every game," Johnny muttered.

Kevin chuckled. "So what do we do, bro? Do we blow the whistle on him?"

"What do you think, Kev?" Johnny asked, eyeing his brother seriously. "We say something, Tanner will be out of the tournament. It'll be that much easier to win."

"Tanner loses the tournament, the endorsement, and his amateur status," Kevin added. "That's his whole life. He'd have to go pro. It'd take him a year to make back what he'd lose on this deal. Plus his name would be mud to other sponsors."

Johnny smiled. "Almost sounds too good to be poetic, huh?"

Kevin nodded. "But if we do that, we don't have to play Tanner in the tournament. And just by the look on your face, I can tell that bugs you."

Johnny didn't answer right away. Then he said, "We can beat him."

A surge of adrenaline pumped through Kevin's system. He'd been thinking the exact same thing. "So what do we do?"

Johnny smiled, his stare wandering over Kevin's shoulder and locking on something. "I think you should ask Penny. Maybe she could talk to her father since he's in the dark about it."

Kevin's eyes narrowed. "What are you talking about? Why would I want to do that?"

"Because she's standing right behind you," Johnny replied.

Johnny left them to begin closing the beach. He had to walk the perimeter, drag furniture back away from the tide's reach, and basically stay out of earshot until Kevin and Penny had time to talk. At least, Kevin hoped he would do that.

"If you want me to leave, I'll leave," Penny offered, speaking softly. Her blue eyes scanned the ocean and the sand; everything but Kevin's face.

Kevin shook his head. "I guess not."

"I can't let it go this way, Kevin," she announced. "I can't let you go thinking what you're thinking of me. I know you have every right to be angry. But you have to believe that I never meant to make you feel less than what you really are." Penny let out a deep breath. "I guess that's what I did with Joe Talbot and the others I dated. I didn't know it at the time because I was too obsessed with getting back at Dad. But you made me see otherwise. Mostly because I've come to care about you. And when you threw it back in my face, it really hurt."

"Good." Kevin didn't want to say it so curtly—and by the look on Penny's face, it stung—but he had to say it. Because it needed to be said. "I'm sorry for being so cold, Penny, but I've come too far to stop telling it like it is. You've been around this fantasy world of wealth and privilege for too long. You don't know what it's like for the other ninety-nine percent of the people in the world. We don't have time to dream up schemes to piss off Dad. We're too busy living life. You should try it sometime."

Penny's eyes darkened. "That's so not fair. Except for one lie, our relationship has been wonderful."

"One major lie," Kevin responded.

"Haven't I treated you with respect?" Penny demanded. "Is that what this is about? Or is it because you think I was kissing you while looking out of the corner of my eye to see who was watching?"

"Were you?" Kevin asked.

Penny laughed bitterly. "I can't believe you would think that of me after the good times we had."

Kevin shook his head in futility. "I just don't know, Penny. Money does such poisonous things to people."

Penny's voice grew so angry that her arms almost flailed. "Once and for all, it's not about the money! I don't care about the money! Do you see me parading around the hotel in a tiara? I've never even had a manicure! Not once! Why do you think I work so hard when I could be trying on clothes in Paris? I hate being under my father's control. He's not real. His world is not real. I don't want that. I want to be real, Kevin. I want to be with people who are real, who know how to treat other people. I want to be with you. Why is that so hard to understand?"

Kevin stepped closer, not flinching. "Because no one inside these hallowed hotel walls thinks like that. From your dad on down the elevator, every person walks in here expecting nothing but luxury and service and five-star butt kissing. And you know why? Because that's what they were raised to expect. The rules are different here, Penny. And you want to break those rules so badly that you're willing to sacrifice everything I'm working for. That's selfish. That's exactly what a rich person would do because that's what they're raised to do. Don't you get it?"

A tear rolled down Penny's cheek, and she swiped it before it could do any more damage. "I get it, all right. I'm apologizing back and forth, Kevin. But you've made this about class. About money. You're lumping me into this big, evil country club where it's all about hurting other people. I can't believe you think I'm like that. Can you look me in the eye and honestly tell me that's what you think?"

Kevin paused. He tried to look her in the eye, and he could manage that. But he knew deep down that Penny truly wasn't like that. Maybe he had done what she said. Maybe he made this about class and about the anger he felt every time he handed over a towel and got a fifty-cent tip.

Maybe he was forgetting the one important thing: that there was a beautiful girl standing in front of him who cared for him and obviously wanted to be with him no matter what the consequences.

But what about Kevin? He cared for her too. She was all he could think about. But was he willing to risk the consequences by taking her back?

"I'm sorry about Dad, Kevin," Penny finally said. "I'm sorry about a lot of things. But I can't make my father stop. That's the one thing I can't do. I think I've finally grown up enough to know that once and for all. If he sees us together, he'll probably kick you out of here. Even if he loses me in the process."

Kevin froze.

Wait a minute . . .

One spark of an idea suddenly hit gasoline in his head, and it took everything for him to keep it under control. But the ideas were raging one after the other.

"Are you serious, Penny?" Kevin asked excitedly.

Penny looked at him oddly. "About what?"

"Could your dad really lose you?" Kevin stared her down. *"Really?"*

"I don't know," she replied. "It's too complicated."

"What I mean is, what if your dad had a good enough reason to let us stay together. Would he do it?"

Penny looked confused. "What are you talking about, Kevin?"

He grinned and abruptly kissed her cheek. "I think I just had a million-dollar idea!" He whirled and called down the beach. *"Yo, Johnny!"*

Penny15: Kevin and I talked today. Finally, really, truly talked. We got everything out in the open and officially forgave each other.

JenniferT: That's so great, Penny! You must be so relieved.

Penny15: For a few seconds it felt like it did that first night with him, everything fresh and new. Like nothing in the world could ever come between us . . .

JenniferT: So you really were serious about this guy from the start. I'm sorry I doubted you.

Penny15: That's all right, Jen. I deserved it. Kevin's changed a lot of things about me. For the better.

JenniferT: So what's the deal with the whole volleyball scandal?

Penny15: Kevin came up with a plan. What he overheard today is illegal. Kevin explained it to me (his brother Johnny picked up on it right away), but I'm still not sure I understand. In the end Kevin asked me to trust him. And I do trust him.

JenniferT: So you don't know what he's going to do about it?

Penny15: No, and I wish I did. Something's on for tonight. There's a big gala ball at the hotel, out by the pool. Black tie. A thousand dollars a plate. A lot of big names will be there. Senators. Movie people. My father. And thanks to me, all three Ford brothers, preparing to hatch Kevin's master plan . . .

JenniferT: IM me tomorrow morning with every detail!

Fourteen

IT WAS A beautiful night.

The stars danced over the hotel patio like Christmas lights. A twelve-piece band played "Girl from Ipanema" over and over. Hundreds of guests milled about, dressed in black tuxedos and luxurious evening gowns that sometimes revealed too much and sometimes, thankfully, not much at all.

A massive buffet table ran a twenty-foot length near the bar, loaded down with shrimp, crab legs, chunk fruit, and caviar. An ice sculpture of a swan, wings spread six feet wide, lorded over the whole scene, looking more like an enraged bird of prey. Melted water dripped off its wings into the pâté.

But the centerpiece had to be the pool. Hundreds of tiny Chinese lanterns floated on the surface, throwing off a surreal yellow-red-blue light that turned people's flesh purple and their teeth gray.

Everyone had a wonderful time, hardly moving at all.

"Who's gonna end up in the pool?" Danny whispered to Kevin as they hovered off to the side—way, way, way off to the side.

"You, if you don't stuff a sock in it," Johnny replied with a grin.

"Oh, like I haven't heard that one before," Danny muttered.

"Guys, hang loose," Kevin said. "Penny said to wait here, so we're waiting here. Don't get us thrown out before we're supposed to be."

"Yeah, we're not exactly dressed for this," Danny commented, tugging on his concert T-shirt.

"Sorry, I left my tux at Salma Hayek's house," Johnny replied. "She insisted on having it dry cleaned after the guacamole incident."

Kevin bristled. "Will you guys knock it off? In case you haven't noticed, we're putting it all on the line here tonight."

Johnny shook his head. "No, little bro, in case you've forgotten, *you're* putting all of *us* on the line tonight. Once again one of my younger, less intelligent siblings has our whole summer hanging by a thread over a girl. I mean, what is it with you two anyway?"

"If this is so bogus," Kevin shot back, "why are you here?"

Johnny sighed. "I'm doing what an older brother is supposed to do: back up my younger brother. That, and I think this plan might actually work." He chuckled. "Besides, I see the look in your eye. I know there will be no peace until you take a shot with this girl."

"And if we get kicked out of the tournament?" Danny asked testily.

Johnny shrugged. "At least that weasel with the Wookiee hair, Tanner, will be just as out on his butt as us. Assuming the plan works, that is."

Danny nodded. "Didn't Dad tell us never to assume anything? Because it makes—"

"We know the cliché," Johnny interrupted. "Watch for the girl."

Penny had led them in from the lobby of the hotel. Kevin did the rest, skirting security by taking his brothers to the far edge of the property, just inside the concrete wall, through some thick landscaping to their spot in an exotic shrub that probably cost more than a year at Yale.

They were supposed to wait for Penny. After that . . . who knew what would happen?

"There's our boy," Danny announced, pointing.

Kevin felt the adrenaline pump harder. It was Tanner. He was dressed in a tieless tux, the kind you might see on Will Smith or Brad Pitt at the Oscars. His hair was blown out over his collar, a well-kept mane that probably took an hour and two assistants to prep. He casually sipped champagne, smiling, grinning, chuckling. The epitome of crass class. His pals, David the hotel marketing director and Fizz Greech, chatted with him like they were all newly minted best buds. Thinking about the contract signing that afternoon made Kevin ill.

"Is he that good?" Kevin wondered aloud.

"You played against him," Johnny replied curtly. "What do you think?"

"I'd like to try him again in daylight," Kevin replied.

"Me too," Danny said.

Johnny laughed. "Amazing. I finally agree with you guys on something."

"Take a Polaroid," Danny grunted.

Just then Kevin spotted Penny. Or at least, a gorgeous young woman who was once Penny but was now transformed into a higher being.

When they'd arrived at the hotel that night, Penny was still dressed in her work whites. She'd escorted them through the lobby in their T-shirts and shorts until Kevin took over the expedition through the landscaped jungle. Penny had said she'd be right back—and it was up to her to get the ball rolling on this master plan.

But Kevin had no idea where she'd gone. Until now. Penny had gone to change her clothes for the party.

She wore a red spaghetti-strap evening gown that almost reached the ground, yet exposed much of her bare back. Her dark hair was pulled back in a tight bun, exposing the smooth white skin of her neck, which displayed a tastefully understated string of pearls.

A lump formed in Kevin's throat. He'd never seen anyone more beautiful in his life.

"Duuuuuuude," Danny marveled. "I finally understand why we're here this evening. Ha. No-brainer, Kev. No-brainer."

"You should see her eyes," Kevin whispered, not taking his own eyes off her.

"I bet," Danny replied, nudging his younger brother.

"Shhh," Johnny ordered. "There she goes."

Penny easily made her way across the patio, not even bothering to see if the Fords were in position. She was cool and elegant and moved with the casual grace of a goddess.

She's so good at this, Kevin thought. *And she's so out of my league.*

Penny casually sidled up to the trio of Tanner, David, and Fizz Greech. She pleasantly interrupted their self-congratulations, and they immediately gaped at this beautiful woman before them. She smiled even wider and pointed back at the hotel, as if directing them somewhere.

The trio's smiles disappeared.

"The bomb is officially dropped," Johnny whispered.

Tanner and David exchanged pained glances. But Penny was ever the lady, smiling and talking as if she were a professional diplomat. Again she pointed at the hotel. Then, her message delivered, she left their group and continued on into the crowd.

Tanner and his cronies shared dark looks. But faced with no other choice—because Kevin knew that the message Penny delivered offered none— the three men straightened their tuxes, put down their drinks, and slowly made their way out of the party and back to the hotel.

"Bull's-eye," Johnny said, smiling. "They took the bait."

"We're not there yet," Kevin reminded him, wiping the sweat from his palms.

Penny wove her way through the crowd, smoothly dodging the greetings and smiles from the guests who knew her. *Probably longtime family friends,* Kevin thought. *People Penny's known her whole life.*

It seemed so alien to him. These people in their tuxes and gowns, with priceless jewelry dripping off them . . . they seemed so *unknowable* to Kevin. But to Penny they were the norm. They were simply people to her. Her father's friends. Kevin and Penny truly came from different worlds.

Kevin swallowed the lump in his throat. This was no time for doubts. He needed to focus on the problem at hand, not the problems he had no control over.

Finally Penny reached her next target: Mr. Booth, her father.

He looked as dapper as ever, a man unchanged from day to day, always dressed for the occasion, always game. He moved like an expert, as Penny did, greeting guests and smiling and making sure that all was always right in his world.

When Penny reached him, he smiled at her too. But Kevin saw a shift in the smile. It was warmer.

Not so guarded. It was the smile a father reserved for his child when he saw how lovely the child had become. When he saw the purity of the moment before the words were spoken: *You look beautiful, my dear.*

But Penny didn't give him the chance. She pulled him close and whispered into his ear.

And the smile immediately evaporated from Mr. Booth's face.

"Fire two," Danny announced. *"Ka-blooie."*

Penny backed away from her father, their mutual stare an unspoken challenge. Who was more stubborn? How far could this charade go?

Penny turned and marched toward the Fords. She spotted them and pointed back at the hotel, as if that was where they should go. She mouthed the words *come on* and passed them. She didn't slow down or offer any other gesture.

"That's our cue," Kevin declared, stepping out of the underbrush, feeling like a blemish with his plain black T-shirt and beat-up shorts. But no one seemed to see them. It was as if they were invisible. That wouldn't last long, he knew. "Let's get a move on, bros."

They followed Penny back to the hotel. Once inside, she stopped to let them catch up. She impatiently waved them forward, glancing left and right as if she expected the Secret Service to pounce on the infidels. Kevin hurried forward but couldn't keep his eyes off her.

"Wow, you look amazing," he whispered when he reached her.

"We don't have time for that," she muttered, though her smirk told a different story. "Get in there. My father will be here in a second." She pointed toward a pair of double doors. The gold-plated sign on the wall said that they were looking at the Los Angeles Room. "The others should be waiting."

Kevin glanced at his brothers, who shrugged.

"Go!" Penny urged.

Kevin nodded and opened the doors. The Los Angeles Room was a large conference room, about twenty feet square. A long table ran the length of the room, surrounded by chairs. More chairs lined the walls. And at the far end of the table, a collective look of shock on their faces, sat Tanner, David, and Fizz Greech.

"What are you clowns doing here?" Tanner demanded.

"Just dropping in to say hello," Johnny replied, smiling. "It's been too long, Tanner. Hey, nice tux."

"You know these boys, Tanner?" Fizz asked, apparently totally confused.

Tanner nodded, sneering. "Just a bunch of bums who want to play in the big time."

"Bums?" Johnny smiled at his brothers. "I guess that means we're in the right room."

David the marketing guy stood up. "Now, what's this all about? We're in the middle of a party—"

"I'd like to know the exact same thing, David," Mr. Booth declared, marching in with Penny at his side. "My daughter seems to think that there's something of great importance going on here." He gave underdressed Kevin and his brothers a cold once-over. "But I can't imagine why she would think that."

"Mr. Booth," David offered, "I have no idea what's going on here. Penny engineered this get-together, but her friends here are obviously not on any guest list. I'll call security."

Penny stepped forward. "No, you won't, Mr. Belfer," she declared, breaking the mystery of David's last name. "Kevin and Johnny Ford are both employees of the hotel, like me. They have just as much right to be here as you do."

Belfer's face grew red. "In T-shirts and shorts? They aren't exactly in proper dress for work."

"My tux is at Salma Hayek's house—," Johnny began, but Kevin nudged him silent.

Penny turned to Mr. Booth. "Dad, you know Kevin is a friend of mine." She threw Kevin a glance. "More than a friend. And you've made your position on that clear. But Kevin's discovered something that you need to know about. Something that has to do with hotel business. So please, listen to him."

Mr. Booth's iron blue eyes focused on Kevin. He took a deep breath, folded his arms, and said, "Okay. I'm listening."

Kevin gulped. This was it. He had to spill his guts and hope he didn't make too much of a mess. But he remained calm, remembering that the worst that could happen was getting booted from the hotel, his job, and the tournament. Ha! A cakewalk.

He cleared his throat and forced his voice to work. "Sir . . . there's a problem with the volleyball tournament."

Belfer stepped forward, wagging a finger. "Mr. Booth, don't listen to this kid. He obviously has an ulterior motive here. Penny said so herself."

Mr. Booth shot Belfer a withering stare. "Sit down, David. You'll get your turn." He glared at Kevin. "Go on."

Kevin waited for Belfer to take his seat. The marketing dude glanced back and forth between Tanner and Fizz, but Kevin couldn't read the emotions. "Anyway," he continued. "The tournament is offering a cash prize but is still open only to amateur competitors, meaning that people like my brother Johnny can play for money without losing any of their college eligibility."

Mr. Booth nodded. "Yes."

"Well, sir, Tanner St. John has signed some kind of endorsement deal with Fizz Cola." Tanner glared nails at Kevin. Kevin stared right back. "See, he's planning on turning pro after the tournament. And Fizz Cola will pay him to endorse their product, the same way any other pro athlete would. On top of that, Mr. Belfer has arranged for the pro volleyball circuit to play several times a year here at the hotel."

"That's a lie!" Belfer exclaimed, standing again.

"No, it's not," Kevin shot back. "I saw Tanner sign the contract today, sir. Any way you slice it,

Tanner St. John is no longer an amateur volleyball player. And from what I heard from Mr. Belfer and Mr. Greech, you don't know anything about this."

Tanner slowly rose from his chair. "You're a dead man, Ford," he whispered. "All of you are dead meat."

"Sit down!" Mr. Booth snapped.

But Tanner didn't sit down. He just stood there, fists balled, chest rising and falling rhythmically. Mr. Booth didn't seem to care. He turned to Belfer. "David, what's the story here?"

Belfer smiled and cleared his throat. "Well, sir, what Kevin is saying . . . What I mean is . . ."

Mr. Booth's words were sharp as knives. "Bottom line. Is it true?"

Belfer blinked, unwilling to answer. Finally, withering under Mr. Booth's stare, he gushed, "Yes, it's all true, Mr. Booth. But I didn't want to bring it to you until it was a slam dunk. Sir, you have to understand just what this deal will be worth to the hotel. I'm talking professional sports in our backyard. Cable-TV coverage, news coverage, and endless exposure for the hotel. We're well-known already, but this deal will bring our hotel to thousands of people, sir. Maybe millions. Add that to the money we make hosting the volleyball, and we can't lose!"

Mr. Booth closed his eyes, shaking his head like a disappointed teacher. Kevin watched as Belfer's expression deflated. That had been his big sell speech. And it didn't fly.

165

"David, I'm at an absolute loss over your actions," Mr. Booth finally said, his voice as serious as a well-aimed rifle. "You know you have no authority to concoct any deal of this magnitude without my knowledge."

"But sir—"

"*I'm* talking now. In the time you have worked here, haven't you learned a thing about how I operate this hotel? I can only imagine that there was some sort of financial incentive for you from Fizz Cola." Mr. Booth shot Greech a vicious glare, but the Fizz man only looked at the floor. "It doesn't matter. What does matter, David, is that I'm running a luxury hotel. A resort. Not the MTV beach house. And not some refugee camp for aspiring ESPN2 commentators. I agreed to the August tournament because it's good business. And because I like supporting young athletes."

Belfer stammered hard, putting up a valiant fight. "S-Sir, if you'll just crunch the numbers . . . If you'll just see what kind of exposure this will bring to the hotel . . ."

"If I wanted exposure, David, I'd advertise on every channel from here to New York One," Mr. Booth retorted. "There is a reason I don't advertise. And there is a reason that this hotel has a ninety-seven percent occupancy rate all year-round without advertising. It's called *reputation,* David. A trait you are suddenly very sorely in lack of. I've spent decades building this hotel's reputation. And I will not sell it off to Fizz Cola or anyone else. Do you understand me?"

Belfer nodded, dejected and defeated. His shoulders drooped like basset-hound ears.

"As for you, Francis," Mr. Booth said, turning to Fizz Greech, "I let you in the door with that tournament sponsorship because it was good business. But you should know better than to try to bypass me. You try it again, and this hotel's relationship with Fizz Cola is over. Do you understand?"

Greech slumped back in his upholstered chair, sending up a huge belch of air. When he finally came to rest, he nodded humbly.

Then Mr. Booth took two steps toward the still-standing Tanner. The volleyball player stood a good two inches over Mr. Booth, but he lost that in courage alone. Kevin saw it in his eyes: defeat, rage, helplessness. Kevin could also see that Tanner wasn't used to these things and didn't like them one single bit.

"You are no longer a guest at this hotel, son," Mr. Booth declared. "You will pack your bags and be out by midnight. Furthermore, I know what this volleyball tournament means to the legitimate amateurs who have signed up to play for a prize that is currently greater than the value of your character. You embraced this backdoor endorsement contract with as much greed as I've ever seen from an athlete. And I've seen 'em all, son. You signed your name to a piece of paper, and now you have to live with it. But not in my hotel and not in my tournament." Mr. Booth leveled a finger of doom. "You're out."

Tanner's eye twitched. "But if I don't play . . . if I don't win the tournament, I don't get any deal. I'm finished without the tournament, sir."

Mr. Booth cocked an eyebrow. "Sounds like you should've had an agent. Live and learn."

With that, Mr. Booth turned away from Tanner, and in that moment Kevin saw the man's real power. Right there, with a matter of a few words, he'd destroyed Tanner St. John. Tanner just stood there, staring into space, the one thing he was best at yanked away like so much candy. He looked ridiculous now, all dolled up in his tux with his blown-out hair. Kevin almost felt sorry for him.

But Mr. Booth was addressing Kevin and his brothers now. "Gentlemen, I am not a fool. Though sometimes people play me for one. You just saw what happens to those people. Kevin, Jake Hackman tells me you're a good employee, one of his best. And you've shown me, at the very least, that you've learned a little bit about how to play this game we call real life. Real life is never fair or impartial."

Here we go, Kevin thought. *The speech. The lecture. How life isn't fair, and too bad, and you and your brothers are out, and if I ever see you in breathing distance of my daughter, you're fish food.*

Booth went on, "You did the right thing. Yes, you used information in your possession to get a leg up, so to speak. But you could have gone about it in some very underhanded ways, and you didn't. You could have gone to the media and embarrassed me and damaged my reputation to no end. You could

168

have played the poor, blue-collar-brothers routine to the hilt and become darlings of the media. You could have blackmailed Tanner or the Fizz people."

Kevin hadn't thought of that one. The Fords could have been multimillionaires if he had! (Just kidding.)

"Furthermore," Booth said, "this whole thing could have blown up on you. I could have been in on it, for all you knew. I could have used this against you to keep you out of the tournament. That said, I thank you for bringing this matter quietly to my attention." Mr. Booth didn't smile. He simply offered his hand to Kevin. "I may have misjudged you, young man."

Kevin blinked, then shook the man's hand. So maybe the plan had worked after all. Earning Booth's respect meant his and Johnny's jobs and the brothers' place in the tourney were secure. Kevin managed to look Mr. Booth in the eye—and he was glad he did. For the first time Kevin saw a human being there. A bright blue twinkle that showed exactly where Penny got her eyes. In them Kevin saw the man, the father, the eventual grandfather. The man who earned a set of rules and played by them no matter what the stakes. In the end, Mr. Booth was that simple.

"Good luck in the tournament, Kevin," he said, giving Kevin's hand one last pump before releasing it. "That goes for you boys too," he added, nodding at Johnny and Danny.

Then the idea hit Kevin so hard, he couldn't

keep his mouth shut. But like Mr. Booth's game of life, this idea seemed right, fair, and under the circumstances absolutely necessary.

"Uh, Mr. Booth?" Kevin asked, stepping forward.

The twinkle in the tycoon's eye was gone. "Yes?"

Kevin glanced at his brothers, who gave him what-are-you-doing stares of horror. But Kevin proceeded.

"Sir, I'd like you to reconsider Tanner's eligibility for the tournament."

The room was dead silent. Eyes grew wide as the words sank in: Johnny's, Danny's, Penny's, and especially Tanner's.

Mr. Booth, however, was nonplussed. "Why?"

Kevin shifted his weight, trying to be confident. "Well, sir . . . to be perfectly honest, the tournament wouldn't be the same without him. He's a great player. *Unfortunately*. And if he doesn't play and we win the tourney, we'll never know if it's because he was out or not. As long as his deal is dead, we have no objection to him playing. In fact, we'd welcome it." Kevin turned to his bros. "Wouldn't we, guys?"

"Uh/um/sure/I guess/yeah/absolutely/let him play/right on . . ."

Kevin turned back to Mr. Booth, smiling. "It really would make for a better tournament, sir. Especially when we beat Tanner's team."

Tanner shot Kevin a look of such intensity that it was impossible to see what he meant: rage? Vengeance? Gratitude? Who knew what the greedy goober was thinking?

Mr. Booth considered this a moment, stroking his jaw. Then a small smile curled his lip. "Done," he said, with a quick nod. He turned to Tanner. "You've just gotten a second chance, young man. And you have Kevin to thank for it. What you do with that chance is entirely up to you."

Tanner nodded lamely, then silently made his way toward the door. Belfer and Greech stood, following him. In seconds the trio was gone without a sound.

"Now," Mr. Booth declared. "I'm neglecting my guests." He turned to leave. "If that's all . . ."

"*Dad,*" Penny blurted out, "that's not even close to all!"

Mr. Booth paused, flinching slightly at his daughter's voice. He turned and smiled pleasantly at her. "What is it, Penny?"

Penny put her hands on her hips. She stared him down, something probably she alone got away with. Kevin felt a wave of butterflies go through him as he watched this gorgeous girl in her best dress take on her greatest adversary.

"What about Kevin?" she demanded.

Mr. Booth looked confused. "What about him?"

"I suppose after all that, you're still going to keep us apart?" Penny asked angrily.

Mr. Booth took a deep breath. "Penny, you know I have only your best interests at heart. I'm sure Kevin has many admirable traits, but for you . . ."

He trailed off. Penny laughed at him. "My best interests? Dad, right now Kevin is my only interest.

171

And if you stand there and compliment him on his admirable qualities while in the same breath telling him he's not good enough for me . . . well, then you're a . . . you're a—hypocrite."

"Penny!" Mr. Booth said, eyes narrowing. "I won't have you talk to me this way in front of these boys."

"Why not?" Penny asked. "Because one's a cabana boy, another's a lifeguard, and one doesn't even have a job? But don't worry, they all still have admirable qualities." Penny shook her head. "Dad, haven't you learned *anything* from tonight?"

"Penny, just because Mr. Ford here is a relatively honest boy doesn't mean he's appropriate for you to date," Mr. Booth pointed out.

"You can tell me exactly what you think is good enough for me," Penny said flatly. "You said Kevin earned your respect, but that's not good enough. So what is? A guy with a nice car? An Ivy League degree? A chain of hotels on the East Coast so you can live your dream of being bicoastal? Would that earn your respect?"

Mr. Booth sighed. "That's enough, Penny."

"Dad, Kevin is as good as any guy gets," she continued. "If you can't see that . . . if you insist on dictating who I see and when I'll see them, what do you think is going to happen when I turn eighteen?"

Mr. Booth scowled.

"Daddy, I love you," Penny said. "I love you so much that I've done some pretty bad things just to get your attention. Like dating guys like Kevin.

Guys with no money or pedigrees. Guys who you would hate on sight. I've dated waiters, cabana boys, pool cleaners, messengers—anyone who'd ensure I'd earn one hour of your time. Don't you see, Dad? I'd rather have you yell at me for an hour than pay no attention to me at all. . . ."

Penny trailed off and looked away. Kevin wanted to rush over to her and hold her. He could tell she was trying to hold back tears.

"I've lost Kevin because of that," she continued. "He thinks the reason I'm interested in him is so I'll make you angry. But he's wrong. I'm interested in Kevin Ford because he's the greatest guy I've ever met."

Penny paused and looked at Kevin. Then she turned back to face her dad. Mr. Booth was staring at her, his face expressionless. "The greatest guy," she went on, "except maybe for you, Daddy."

And that's when Mr. Booth's face cracked. He held out his arms, and Penny flew into them.

Kevin glanced at his brothers. Johnny and Danny were looking at the floor out of respect for the privacy and intimacy this moment called for between father and daughter.

"I'll never be ready for you to turn eighteen," Mr. Booth said, his voice emotional. "I guess I'm not as good with the nurturing-mother part as I am at the overprotective-father part, am I? Sometimes I forget that it's just you and me, Penny. I'm reminded of your beauty every day, but sometimes I forget how quickly you've grown up on the inside too. In fact, it's rather frightening that you can teach me a thing or two." He smiled at Penny and ran a finger along her cheek.

Then he turned to Kevin, and the stern look returned to his face. "Kevin, you have my blessing to see my daughter. I think you understand that she's my real wealth in this life. Treat her accordingly."

Kevin nodded sharply. "I will, sir."

Penny's grin was wide as the Pacific. She flung her arms around her father's neck and gave him the hug of the year. "Oh, Dad, I'm so proud of you!"

Mr. Booth grinned too and broke into laughter. "Ah, at last the tables are turned, sweetheart. Because I've always been proud of you."

Kevin beamed and shared a look of relief with his brothers. Johnny responded by giving Kevin a good-natured punch on the arm.

The Booths broke their embrace, and Penny grabbed Kevin's hand. He thought that he could just about spend eternity in those bright blue eyes. Or at least a summer.

Mr. Booth clapped and rubbed his hands. "Now . . . is there anything else before I return to my party?" he asked in mock exasperation.

No one said anything at first.

But then Danny's voice piped up from behind Kevin. "Well . . . I need a job."

Fifteen

OUTSIDE, THE NIGHT air was cool and breezy. The party rolled on, the band played "New York, New York," and the world continued to spin.

Johnny clapped a hand on Kevin's shoulder. "Well, bro, you pulled it off. All I can say is, you are *soooo* lucky you didn't screw this up for us."

Kevin chuckled. "Hey, what can I say—I'm a master of disaster. But thank Penny. She's the one with the connections."

"And the smarts, apparently," Danny added.

Penny laughed. "That's a mighty high compliment coming from a newly minted cabana boy."

Danny shrugged. "Hanging around all those giants of the business world made me realize that when presented with an opportunity, you have to be quick or be dead."

"Wasn't that in a Rodney Dangerfield movie?" Kevin mused.

"I don't care if it was in a fortune cookie," Johnny declared, "as long as Kramer here can hold down a steady job for the rest of the summer."

Danny gave Kevin a playful shove. "If Kevin can be a cabana boy, then anyone can."

"Ain't that the truth," Kevin muttered.

Johnny sighed. "Well, bro, we'd like to hang out, but I've gotta go. I have some mandatory night-swimming seminar to go to. And I promised my partner, Kylie, I'd pick her up."

"Does Jane know you're picking up female life-guards in hot bathing suits for night swims?" Danny asked.

Johnny made a shut-up and yeah-right-like-I'd-ever face, but Kevin wondered. Johnny had been seeing Jane, his girlfriend from back home, *forever*. Could some other girl nab Johnny away? Kevin doubted it. But after this whole experience with Penny, Kevin had learned not to doubt *anything*.

"I've gotta split too," Danny said. "I'm meeting Raven in front of Jabba's."

Penny grabbed Kevin's hand and gave it an urgent squeeze. "You're not leaving, are you?"

Kevin looked at Penny, the flowing red dress, the luminous blue eyes, the playful smile. Man, he was the luckiest cabana boy on the face of the earth. "No, not now." He turned to his brothers. "Don't wait up for me, boys. The party is just starting."

"Just don't embarrass us," Johnny replied, gesturing at the party goers. "There's a lot of opinion makers in there. Can't have them thinking ill of the Ford family."

"I'll do my best," Kevin replied.

With that, Johnny and Danny disappeared. Kevin turned to Penny, eyebrows raised. "Now what? They're right—I'm not dressed for this."

Penny smiled and slid her arms around his neck. Her lips moved within inches of his. "I don't care. I've never cared. You could be in a burlap sack, and I'd still ask you to dance, right here, right now."

Kevin smirked. "What if I said no?"

Penny laughed. "Then security would see how far they could throw you."

"I guess I'll say yes." They slowly moved to the music, the full horn section blasting across the patio. Kevin inhaled Penny's sweet scent and gently pulled her closer. She didn't object.

They danced like that in silence, Kevin simply enjoying Penny's presence. Enjoying the fact that they didn't have to hide anymore. He could feel the stares of the party guests, most of them wondering, *Who is that dirtbag dancing with the host's daughter?*

The thought made Kevin smile.

Then someone tapped his shoulder. Hard.

Kevin turned to see Tanner. Actually, he saw Tanner's tux shirt. He had to look up to see his face. A bolt of adrenaline raced through Kevin. Why was Tanner still here? And what would he do in the middle of a party like this?

"You're not supposed to be here," Penny said sharply.

"Just take it easy," Tanner growled, holding up a hand. "I've got something to say to you, Ford."

177

Kevin forced himself to meet Tanner's stare. *Don't back down, don't back down.* "Yeah?"

"I'm not going to apologize for anything," Tanner said. "But thanks is all you get for getting me back in the tournament. I know the only reason you did it was to look good for her old man. But still . . . thanks." His stare dripped contempt at the mention of the word. "Just remember, this doesn't change anything between us. We're still going to humiliate you out there. We're going to hurt you." He poked Kevin's chest. "Remember that."

"Whatever, dude," Kevin replied.

Tanner poked him once more for emphasis, then slowly turned away and disappeared into the crowd.

"What a jerk," Penny whispered.

"A jerk with a hundred-mile-an-hour spike," Kevin replied. "That tournament is going to be very interesting."

"You'll win," Penny said, her tone so confident that Kevin almost laughed.

"I wish it was that simple."

"Let's dance, Kevin," she said gently. "That doesn't take so much effort."

Kevin smiled and pulled her close once more. Then he let out a deep breath over her shoulder. "Wow, so we're allowed to do this in public. Anytime, anywhere we want. Feels good, huh?"

"Very good," she replied softly, hugging him close.

Kevin couldn't help but smile. "So, maybe my new pal Austin Booth will drive you up the four hours to come visit me once summer ends."

"He just might," Penny said. "And maybe Johnny will drive you down." They drew apart long enough to gaze at each other and share a perfect kiss.

They continued their dance under the glow of the Chinese lanterns and summer stars, an ordinary guy in shorts and a beautiful princess in a red gown. And Kevin knew deep down, without a doubt, that they were the best-matched couple in the house.

Do you ever wonder about falling in love? About members of the opposite sex? Do you need a little friendly advice but have no one to turn to? Well, that's where we come in . . . Jenny and Jake. Send us those questions you're dying to ask, and we'll give you the straight scoop on life and love.

DEAR JAKE

Q: *I have a gigantic problem. My best friend (I'll call her Jade) told me that she likes a guy at school and that she's going to try to hook up with him. You know, flirt with him, hang out with him, whatever. The prob is this: I've liked this guy for a while and was keeping it to myself because I didn't think I'd have a chance with him. I mean, it's possible he'd like me, but I don't know. . . . So if Jade goes after him and he likes her, I'll be so jealous! Should I tell her that I like him too? That I liked him first?*

MS, Boulder, CO

A: This is a toughie. I think the best thing to do is to keep quiet—at least for now. Your friend spoke up and announced her plan to go after this guy, so she's sort of got dibs on trying to hook up with him. If they become a couple, sure, you'll be jealous. But I'm sure you'll also be happy for your best friend. Before you know it, you'll like someone else. And if they don't become a couple, maybe after some time has passed, you can fess up to your friend and tell her you always liked him too. Depending on her response, maybe you'll finally try to hook up with him yourself.

Q: *I came home a little early from school today and found my mom snooping in my dresser drawers! She said she was just putting away some clean laundry, but my journal was in the drawer she was poking around in. She said she didn't read it. But what if she did? I'd be mortified! How can I keep her out of my room?*

KA, Paramus, NJ

A: Well, you can't. From the sounds of it, your mom does respect your privacy. She said she didn't read your journal, so why not believe her? A lot of people keep journals—your mom may keep one too. And I'm sure she wouldn't want you or anyone else peeking in it. Give her the benefit of the doubt. And thank her for not only doing your laundry but putting it away!

DEAR JENNY

Q: *I have a crush on a guy who's a year younger than me. He's in eighth grade, and I'm in ninth, so he's not even in high school yet! My friends would laugh in my face if they knew I liked a guy in middle school. I should just forget him, right?*

JJ, Dallas, TX

A: As if you could! And who says your friends would laugh? If you like him, they'd probably understand why you do. Give them some credit—they just might surprise you. And you'll be free to pursue your crush without worry!

Q: *I've been seeing someone for a month, and everyone at school knows we're boyfriend and girlfriend. The problem is, I don't really like him. He's sort of obnoxious, and he's not as smart as I thought he was. He's sort of popular, though, and I've made more friends because of him. Should I just keeping going out with him?*

CB, Syracuse, NY

A: Sure, if you could stand it—and yourself. Dating someone because it'll make you popular or get you something is unfair to the person and to you. Wouldn't you rather date someone you like? And doesn't your boyfriend deserve to date someone who thinks he's great?

Do you have any questions about love?
Although we can't respond individually to your letters,
you just might find your questions answered in our column.

Write to:
Jenny Burgess or Jake Korman
c/o 17th Street Productions,
an Alloy Online, Inc. company.
33 West 17th Street
New York, NY 10011

Don't miss any of the books in *Love Stories*
—the romantic series from Bantam Books!

Turn up the **heat** and the

volume!

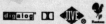